HINNOM MAGAZINE

August 2017
ISSUE 002

Edited by C.P. Dunphey

Gehenna & Hinnom Books

Table of Contents:

Introduction by C.P. Dunphey   1

ENQUIRIES FROM THE ABYSS:
Interview with T.E. Grau   5

Featured Story:
Godmouth by P.L. McMillan   17

The Black Dog by Max D. Stanton   43
Death Carriage by Matthew Penwell   59
The Little Dead Thing by John S. McFarland   69
Vessel by Ibai Canales   93
Dry Bones by Charles D. Shell   109
The Nocturne of Manigault by Joanna Costello   123
Nothing but Dans, All the Way Down by
Konstantine Paradias   147
The Power of Hate by Hugh McStay   163
Spidering Down an Alley by Jeff Johnson   173

Reprint:
Last of the Aztec Riders by Mark Mellon   191

OATS Studios Volume 1—A Gehenna Post Review
Series   205

Celebrating the Unknown

Introduction
by C.P. Dunphey

Welcome to Gehenna & Hinnom.

127 years ago, a man was born in Providence, Rhode Island, that would go on to not only influence authors such as Stephen King and directors like Guillermo Del Toro, but who would also inspire generations of filmmakers and writers so profoundly, that his effects on popular culture would be eternal, whether most people recognized it or not. Howard Phillips Lovecraft was born on August 20th, 1890, in Providence to his father, Winfield Scott Lovecraft and his mother, Sarah Susan Phillips Lovecraft. His early childhood was wrought with nightmares, illness, and tragedy. Winfield died in 1898 after being institutionalized when Lovecraft was only three years of age, his mother following suit and similarly being institutionalized for insanity in the same hospital, several years later.

Many of the horrifying tales Lovecraft would later go on to write were cited as inspirations from his nightmares he experienced as a child. A high school dropout and, by all cultural standards at the time, a failure, Howard Phillips Lovecraft was never expected to succeed. Even around the time of his death, due to intestinal cancer, in 1937, Lovecraft felt that he had not succeeded in his own right as an author. Thanks to August Derleth and many other friends of the late author, this fortunately was never the reality of which Lovecraft expected.

H.P. Lovecraft is credited with creating the genre of Cosmic Horror, or, horror of the unknown. He famously stated in his now-legendary essay, "Supernatural Horror in Literature," that, "The oldest and strongest emotion of mankind is fear, and the oldest and strongest kind of fear is fear of the unknown." No other author has ever capitalized on this notion and executed fiction around this concept quite as astutely as Lovecraft did. His stories beg the reader to dive into the unknown, the very fabric of our fears and the very limitations of our knowledge thereof.

Over the past several years, Lovecraft and Cosmic Horror have become staples in the darker genres of literature, solidifying the late author as an authority in the fields of horror, and perhaps one of the greatest American writers to have ever lived. It would be foolish to denounce or deny the impact of Lovecraft's bibliography, and the foundations in which he built for many authors of the future. Lovecraft's Cthulhu Mythos are a constantly-expanding universe in which authors of old and new can explore, and more importantly, craft their own innovations within.

Gehenna & Hinnom was founded with the principles of adhering to a standard of dark literature, welcoming the very genres that so often become undermined by scholars and mainstream writers. Science Fiction, Horror, and Fantasy—all genres in which Lovecraft dabbled and birthed his creations—are just as important to culture as Romanticism or Tragedy. It took 100+ years for people to truly start respecting Lovecraft, even after his plethora of contributions to the genres we hold so dear. We move forward, into the future, with the hope that the talented, wonderful writers of today's dark literature, will not go unnoticed or underappreciated.

We invite you all to Embrace the Unknown.

"Searchers after horror haunt strange, far places."

—H.P. Lovecraft
"The Picture in the House" December 12th, 1920

Enquiries from the Abyss:

An Interview with Dark Fiction author T.E. Grau

(Originally published in The Gehenna Post)

Greetings from the Ethereal Plane,

In dark fiction, there are many voices who have clambered their ways into the skulls of readers. Though the influx is large, it is rare for one of these voices to nestle into the consciousness of readers in the way that T.E. Grau's work has accomplished. He who the Gehenna Post has named, "Dark Fiction's Most Promising Young Voice." We began a review series for Grau's work, reviewing both his Shirley Jackson Award-nominated collection, *The Nameless Dark*, and his novella, *They Don't Come Home Anymore*. Grau has been paving his way steadily and meticulously into the realm of dark fiction, crafting unforgettable fiction along the way. His new release, *I Am The River* from Lethe Press will release in February of 2018. While we await the next chapter in Grau's stunning resume of horror and dark fiction, let's dive in to the unknown and learn where his newest piece will take us.

CP: You have burst onto the Dark Fiction scene with much praise and the anticipation for your new work, *I Am the River*, is well-deserved. As an author, voices such as Laird Barron and Adam Nevill have praised your work.

Could you describe for our readers the steps that your career has progressed in recent years? What aspirations and goals do you have for the future?

TE: I'm so grateful for the support of fellow writers. That was very important in allowing me to get my first collection published by Lethe Press, as I was mostly unknown to the publisher until my work was recommended online by Nathan Ballingrud (who graciously agreed to write the introduction to *The Nameless Dark*), and Laird Barron. Once the collection found a home, the blurbs I asked for and received from major names in horror and dark fiction around the world still blow me away. I was treated very kindly by so many colleagues and authors I admire, including Adam, and I'll never forget that.

Following the release of *The Nameless Dark*, the critical feedback was thankfully positive, and the collection received a nomination for a Shirley Jackson Award. That led to an increase in offers to release my work with various publishers. I agreed to a publishing deal with This Is Horror to publish my next project, which became the novella *They Don't Come Home Anymore*, taking us up to the present, and a few larger projects on which I'm currently working. It wasn't planned this way, but each successive book has grown in terms of size and scope, as the collection reflected short stories and novelettes, *They Don't Come Home Anymore* was a novella, and my current project, *I Am The River*, will certainly be a novella, and might grow itself into an outright novel. I'll know more in late August when I finish the book.

In terms of future goals, I want to write my proper novel ("proper," in terms of planning it to be novel-length from the start) *Salt Creek*, and finish and release a second collection or short fiction (title and cover already set and secured, but not released at the moment). Beyond that, I'll write what appeals to me, and see where it all fits.

CP: You spoke of authors treating you very well when you burst onto the scene, even those you admire. For our readers, who are mostly authors themselves, what about connections and friendships creates such a strong bond that helps authors like yourself catapult into the mainstream? How would you recommend other authors learn from this historical style of camaraderie (E.g. The Lovecraft Circle)?

TE: Well, I'm certainly not in the mainstream, but I do appreciate the vote of confidence.

Writing is like any creative scene, in that it runs on talent and relationships, and talent creating relationships with each other. Helping each other, creating something larger than oneself, sort of like an unofficial union or guild. Strength in numbers. I believe in things like this, although I also realize that it's very rare when this actually happens, as self-interest and other issues usually— pardon the pun—trump generosity, cooperation, and support.

That said, camaraderie is important. Supporting other writers and their work is important. Essential, even. Paying forward to newer and emerging writers the support and assistance you have and continue to receive is important. I've tried to do that as much as I can, within my means.

A supportive community can grow great things. For example, Seattle became the mecca of music in the early 90s because most of the bands knew, supported, and jammed with each other. They were a scene, and when the big labels came calling, a lot of them got a shot. That's powerful, as a scene draws interested eyes, while a collection of scattered individuals sometimes makes it difficult for gatekeepers to target and pin down, and often more trouble than it's worth, as they don't have the time or the understanding to do the necessary work to uncover the gems that can and will change the cultural landscape.

This needs to happen in the writing community, and has, to a point. More is necessary, though. No one will care if we don't care ourselves.

CP: It is very notable that, as an author, you have a distinct ability to craft narratives that differ in each story/work. Many writers maintain a voice that is consistent, often choosing genres and themes that are similar in style. Most of your stories are incomparable, standing on their own and independent of one another. How did this ability develop and what inspired you to be such a versatile writer?

TE: I'm not really sure how this developed, but I suppose it might come from my interest in so many things, including history, geography, astronomy, religion, sociology, race, family, and gender dynamics, and the occult, and a mild faculty for vocal mimicry. These interests show themselves in the stories I write, as I like to write about what interests me.

I also think that certain stories should/could be told in certain style, or in a certain setting, that might not be commonplace or similar to my other stories. Texture, tempo, and rhythm can vary, based on the influencing factors of character(s), location, time period, and the underlying messages (if any) in the piece.

I'm not a musician (that broken down ship sailed long ago), but I imagine that it's similar to what songwriters experience when writing a song, in that how it sounds is based in large part on what the song is about, and the purpose of the song being written.

CP: You have been nominated for the Shirley Jackson award for Best Single-Author Collection, among many other accomplishments. What event or moment, as an author, was your proudest? What do you feel was the turning point for you as a writer?

TE: I was most proud when my wife and daughter held my collection in their hands for the first time as a finished, published book. That somehow made it all real, that I had finally accomplished something substantial as a writer after doing it for most of my life. Secondarily, seeing a book I had written on a library shelf for the first time was very, very satisfying. I felt like a tiny, miniscule part of the larger literary body. I've always been in awe of writers, books, and libraries, and now I could finally join myself to that stream of cultural permanence.

There are two major turning points in my career as a writer. The first was when my wife Ivy encouraged me to stop writing screenplays and write prose, which is what I secretly always wanted to do anyway. The next was a feeling that I should—and could—stop writing homage fiction or pastiche and write my own stories in my worlds. Lovecraftian fiction served as an entry point into writing short stories, as it gave me an avenue to frame my work and get it published in Lovecraft—or Cthulhu-themed—anthologies, and I'm very grateful for that. But after I found my legs, I realized I could trudge up on the mountain on my own two feet. I think many writers of dark and horror fiction have followed a similar route into realizing their own individuality as an author, going back to the 1930s, so I'm certainly not alone in this regard. Regardless of what I write going forward, or my personal feelings about the man, I'll always owe Lovecraft a debt of gratitude for opening up his multiverse to be plundered by others, which allowed uncertain writers like me to grab onto his coattails and hitch a ride into the meeting room.

CP: As we have noted in both our reviews for *The Nameless Dark* and *They Don't Come Home Anymore*, respectively, there are notable influences in your writing, primarily Lovecraftian and Liggoti-esque for your collection, and what we found to be thematic material relative to Stephen King's early work. Were we accurate with these suggestions? If not, who has inspired you as an author?

TE: Lovecraft is certainly an influence, especially in my earlier work, as touched upon above. Ligotti is also an influence, I think, although it's tough to tell. Knowing the difference between writers that have directly influenced the way I write in a discernable way and those who I admire greatly is difficult to determine, at least by me. Tonally, Ligotti is an inspiration, to be sure.

I don't see King as an influence, although it's certainly possible, as I have read a lot of his work throughout my life, and certainly in the last five years. I don't see many similarities between he and I, although we probably share many of the same influencing factors. I adore King, both as a person and a writer.

My main influences—those that I can see and feel—are Hunter S. Thompson, Jack Kerouac, and Lovecraft. Authors that I have read and admire and from which I draw inspiration include Ligotti, Flannery O'Connor, Ray Bradbury, Toni Morrison, T.E.D. Klein, William Faulkner, Willa Cather, Lawrence Block, and Cormac McCarthy, to name a few.

CP: Concerning themes, could you delve into *I Am The River* a little? How will it be different from your previous outings?

TE: *I Am The River* will be my longest work to date, and is different in that the point of view changes from first person to third throughout the story. The protagonist is an African American veteran of the Vietnam War, hiding out in Bangkok five years after the war, unable to return home as he works through the horrors he has seen and unleashed, and the dark presence that haunts him on a daily basis, which often comes to him as the hound Black Shuck. The story deals with the nature of war and the impact of those who fight, endure, and survive it, sleep paralysis, PTSD in a time before it was diagnosed or even recognized as a legitimate side effect of trauma, the processing and resolution of guilt, anger, and fear, and the covert—and often incredibly strange—psychological operations carried out during the Vietnam War by the CIA and other agencies in an attempt to win a war that we were clearly losing, contrary to every battle assessment, body count, and press release.

I get to explore lots of things in this book that I haven't fully dealt with before, and it provides me a chance to write about a misunderstood war that inflicted—and continues to inflict—so much physical and psychological damage on so many people on so many sides, including my own father, who fought in Vietnam.

CP: Concerning *I Am The River*, a 1990 film that is—still to this day—very underrated, comes to mind. Adrian Lyne's *Jacob's Ladder*. Going on to inspire franchises like *Silent Hill*, the film delved into the psychological experiments conducted during Vietnam. Why do you think this topic is so heavily ignored and what inspired you to explore its reality in your writing? How will your novella differ from previous portrayals of the events?

TE: The baseline elements—PTSD, sleep paralysis, and a particularly strange and totally real PSY-OP program created during the Vietnam War—were brought to me by a filmmaker who was interested in developing a film project that explored these concepts. He'd read my work, and first approached me to adapt one of my published stories for the screen, which he is doing right now. In the meantime, he asked if I could come up with a story that included those particular elements without any direction relating to story and character, and what I created is *I Am The River*. So, in a sense, it's a commissioned piece, in a very loose definition of the term, although all of the characters, settings, and plot are my own.

I've never seen *Jacob's Ladder*, but from what I know of the plot, there aren't many similarities other than the shared setting of the Vietnam War, and the use of flash-backs. The PSY-OP in my story isn't an experiment, it was an actual program created to deliver terror to the enemy drawing on their belief in the supernatural. That's all I'll say about that for now.

As for why this topic is routinely ignored, I really have no idea, other than many of those who fought in Vietnam don't seem too eager to talk about it, so it's up to dummies like me born after it was over to attempt an interpretation of what happened there.

CP: It says on your Amazon author page that you are currently working on another collection and your first novel. What are the plans for these works? Do you prefer longer or shorter pieces? Why?

TE: My second collection should be a varied work, showing where I am now as a reader and writer, which is a bit different than where I was seven years ago. I want to do something interesting with the presentation of the book, as well, and am working with my wife on several ideas to make it something of an "enhanced" print edition.

My novel *Salt Creek* is probably best described as *The X-Files* meets Willa Cather with a touch of *Twin Peaks*. In it, I'll explore the "lost" town and geographic region of Salt Creek, Nebraska, a peculiar place named for a salt water stream in the middle of the prairie that doesn't appear on any maps, but is—at least from time to time—quite real. Salt Creek features heavily in my novelette *The Mission*, and is nodded to in a few other stories. The novel will help further the mythos and well-hidden history of the place, and build on it for this and future works.

Regarding my preference for shorter or longer pieces, I like both, as some stories should be told briefly, giving just a glimpse of an ongoing world, while others demand a longer, more thorough investigation. The story itself will tell you how large or small it wants to be, provided that you listen closely and stay true to the guiding spirit of the tale. Stories never lie, unless they're forced to do so.

CP: The technique of authors using world building for short fiction, connecting several of their stories to the same central universe, seems to be at an all-time high in popularity—whether it be a single author or several operating within the same realm of fiction—with the massive resurgence in Lovecraftian popularity. How did the setting of Salt Creek come to be a place that you used for multiple stories? Why is world building just as important for short fiction as it is for longer works?

TE: Going back to my first days of writing prose and horror fiction, I wanted to create my own reality, build my own version of our world, inspired by contemporary writers like Ramsey Campbell (Severn Valley), Jeffrey Thomas (Punktown), Laird Barron (the Old Leech mythos) and W. H. Pugmire (Sesqua Valley), among others, all of whom crafted new universes in which to house many of their stories. This was appealing to me, especially as a kid who grew up reading high fantasy fiction, where so many novels were set in specific realities created for those books and characters. Places like Krynn, Prydain, Middle Earth, Forgotten Realms, and the lands of the Belgariad and the Hyborian Age were as real to me as anything on an actual map. That left a powerful impression.

In creating Salt Creek, I decided early on to build out this familiar but slightly askew world in the Sandhills of Nebraska, which is a strange, bleak, and sometimes beautiful place, although future tales will expand the "network" into connected locations in California, Pennsylvania, and other areas across the globe. I'm very much looking forward to pulling more real estate from the void as my writing continues.

World building obviously isn't essential, and can become a crutch, but it's also incredibly fun, ceding more architectural power to a writer, and providing an efficient way to frame a series of stories, characters, and locations in one unique universe where the rules bow to the discretion of the creator. To answer your last question, I think world building is just as important for short fiction as longer works because short fiction is just as important, in general, as longer works. More so, sometimes, as some of the best and most effective works of fiction, for my money, are short stories, not novels.

CP: On a closing note, we always try to have a final question that relates to helping young and aspiring authors tread their paths. Hearing advice from writers one admires is often a very powerful tool that can benefit new authors enormously with their own trajectories and career paths. If you had to give one single strand of advice to a young author, what would it be? And why?

TE: Whenever I'm asked this question my answer is always the same—read more than you write.

Consider yourself an athlete, where training and practice time far exceeds the time spent performing in an actual contest. Hundreds, even thousands, of accumulated training hours go into one three hour game or match. Think of boxers, martial artists, football and basketball players. Think of long distance runners, who log hundreds and hundreds—even thousands—of miles to train for a race that is never longer than 26.2.

The same can be said for writers, with reading as their training. The act of writing is also training, obviously, but more resembles an end result contest than practice. However, that foundational repetition of the fundamentals that leads to the best athletic performance (ball handling in basketball and soccer, route running in football, batting practice in baseball, etc.) can only be achieved through reading, and reading far afield from normal habits and comfort zones, taking in the best literature this world has produced, and breaking it down inside your head, absorbing traces of its DNA, and then hopefully synthesizing this fuel when you write your own work. It's absolutely essential to becoming a good, and a better, writer. Uncultivated natural ability will only take you so far. Training, discipline, and hard work will take you the rest of the way.

GODMOUTH

by P.L. McMillan

The first time I heard it was from a dying woman's lips. She'd been hit by a car that had been going at least double the speed limit. The driver hadn't stopped. Instead, the car had squealed around a corner and disappeared as the woman slammed into the ground with a sickening *crunch*. I saw it happen, as did four other strangers.

I ran to the woman's side as she lay dying. I knew she had to be. I was a nurse and the amount of blood surrounding the woman on the pavement was gruesome. I heard a man on his cellphone, talking to the 911 dispatch.

The other strangers stood a little ways away, watching as I checked her vitals and tried to make her comfortable. Her eyes were a beautiful shade of the palest green, reflecting the stormy sky above. She wasn't upset or crying. I thought that she must be in shock.

"Miss, an ambulance is coming," the man on the cellphone said, raising his voice to avoid coming closer.

I nodded.

"Did you hear that? Just hold on, you'll be okay," I lied, pressing my scarf against the deep gash on her scalp.

Half of her forehead had been scraped up and into her hairline from her collision with the pavement. Her skull glistened. Her lips moved but I couldn't hear any sound coming from them. Her eyes never left the sky. In the distance, I heard the insistent wail of an ambulance. I leaned in, turning my head so my ear was closest to her mouth. I heard the faint whisper of the breath, she was trying to say something. The ambulance screamed through the streets.

"Is there anything I can do? Is she going to be alright?" a woman asked, clutching her coat around her and staring at me with wide, frightened eyes.

I shook my head and turned back to the dying woman. I started. She was staring right at me. Her manicured hand clutched at my sleeve and she smiled. I leaned in, meaning to comfort her.

"God mouth," she said.

She died then. Her fingers slipped from my sleeve to land in her blood, which was reflecting the sky as her eyes did once more. There was a contented smile on her lips.

"May she rest in peace," said another woman, shaking her head.

"Such a shame," said the woman clutching her coat.

"Did anyone get that asshole's license plate?" said the man.

The ambulance roared around the corner and rolled to a stop nearby. I stood and stepped away from the dead woman as the EMTs jumped out of the back. The others and I stood and watched them try to resuscitate her. It wasn't long before they gave up and put the body on a stretcher and covered those blank eyes with a blanket.

The women crept closer, their eyes latched onto the still figure underneath the cover. The EMTs called in the death. A police car finally rolled up.

"What did she say to you?" asked one of the women.

"Did she know that asshole in the car?" asked the other.

I shook my head.

"God mouth," I said.

"God?" repeated the first woman.

"She was praying," said the other.

Satisfied, the women drifted off together to talk to the police. I thought about what they had said. It hadn't sounded like a prayer.

By the time I had finished giving my statement and information to the police, it was growing late. I watched the police car and ambulance slowly pull away, all the strangers and watchers turned and wandered away as well.

Only the blood pool on the pavement remained. I stared at the reflection of the clouds on the blood, at my stained scarf lying next to it, before turning my back against it all and walking back home.

The next time, I didn't hear it. Rather I saw it written on the side of a building in egg yellow spray paint next to a crude representation of a wide, open mouth with square teeth inside. It was written all as one word:

GODMOUTH

I caught sight of it as I was walking to the hospital. I stopped at the mouth of the alley and stared into the shadows. It'd been written at chest height, above some dented trashcans. It was the first time I thought about that woman in two days.

I took out my phone and stepped into the alley, trying to avoid the puddles of vomit and piss, garbage and what looked suspiciously like human shit. I didn't know why but I wanted a picture of the graffiti. After I snapped two photos of it, I stood and stared at it. A chill come over me as I remembered the dead woman's smile and the way her beautiful green eyes had reflected the clouds, how she had whispered that final word in such a calm and loving way.

I was brought back to the present by the stench of a homeless man who had come up behind me.

"Spare a dollar for a homeless vet?" he coughed into his dirty hands before holding one out to me.

I dug a couple dollars out of my coat pocket and handed them to him, escaping as his attention was turned to counting them out. I drew my new scarf tighter around my neck and hurried down the sidewalk, dodging the business men and women in fashionable clothes as they left work.

I reached the hospital a few minutes late and my supervisor chewed me out as I got into my scrubs. I followed my boss out as she continued her rant.

"I can't have my nurses coming in late. You know how hectic and swamped we can be. I expect more from you, you're one of the best nurses I have," Ellen said as she charged down the crowded hallway, "things have been crazy these last few weeks, you should know better."

"I'm sorry, Ellen. I won't let it happen again."

"No, you won't," she replied, shoving a clipboard at me.

I looked over the counter of the nurse's station at the crowded waiting room. All the seats were taken and even more people were leaning against the walls or slouching in groups near the entrance.

"No time to just stand around," Ellen said as she sat down in the chair behind the counter and began to sort through the forms there.

I turned and went back down the hall to where the elevators were. The elevator dinged just as I pressed the 'up' button. I stood aside as Jimmy, a night orderly, wheeled out an old man. The gentleman was withered, slouched over his lap with thick ropes of drool dangling from his mouth. He smelled distinctly of urine and, from the dark patch on his crotch, it was obvious where the smell was coming from. Jimmy saw my expression and nodded.

"Yeah, I'll clean him up. It happened on the way down and I need to get him to the MRI. He was fine an hour ago, talking about politics. So bizarre."

The old man began to rock back and forth. I saw a smile on his face and then he said it:

GODMOUTH

I started and stared. "What did he say?"

Jimmy looked down at the smiling, drooling old man and shrugged.

"I don't know what it means, he just keeps saying it. Probably just a side effect of the stroke he had or whatever it is that caused this." Jimmy lifted a hand in a wave as he pushed the wheelchair down the hall and away from me.

Staring after them, I stepped onto the elevator and pressed the button for the fifth floor. Ellen was obviously pissed at me since she had given me the worst night duty to cover; the psych ward. Normally this was covered by the resident psych doctors but, with budgets cuts, it had been relegated to the nurses. On the bright side, they usually always assigned two nurses to take care of the patients since some of them could be violent.

Alison was already behind the counter on the fifth floor, waiting for me to arrive so we could start the rounds. Alison was my favourite person to be teamed up with. She was forty but acted like she was still in college, cracking dirty jokes and partying on her days off. Ellen hated her, which is why Alison often worked the night shift on the fifth floor. She smirked at me when she caught sight of me.

"Guess who got lucky last night?" she asked by way of a hello.

I rolled my eyes but couldn't help smiling.

"Let's see to our guests and you can tell me all about it," I replied.

She filled me in on all the sticky details as we walked the bright halls to the backdrop of whimpering, screaming, and hissed one-sided conversations. I hated this floor so much.

We rounded the final corner and she took the left side, I took the right. We peeked in the windows, checking to make sure everyone was in bed, or at least, accounted for. Most of these people weren't too unstable, just some mild schizophrenia and paranoia.

Occasionally, they could get violent but neither of us would be actually going into the rooms. I was checking the third room when I froze. The patient, Walter Carlson, was asleep with his back to me. Above his bed, scrawled in big, blocky letters was the word that had been haunting me:

GODMOUTH

Worse, the words were wet looking and red. I must have gasped because Alison was immediately at my side.

"Oh Jesus, Mary, and Joseph. Is that blood?"

"I think so," I said.

"Fuck me, is he dead? That's a lot of blood. Is he breathing? Can you tell if he is breathing?"

I squinted through the window but shook my head.

"We have to go in there," I said.

"I'm calling security."

Alison darted down the hall to the nurse's station.

I found my hand on the doorknob before I realized what I was doing. I listened to Alison arguing on the phone. I stepped inside the room, leaving the door open behind me so the hall light could shine further into the room. The words glared out through the shadows, gleaming in the faint light. Inside the room, I saw that the opposite wall had been marked as well.

The crude mouth drawing, exactly the same as the one in the alley, had been dabbed onto the wall with more blood. This drawing was larger though and I could make out that the teeth were long and stretched down past the lower lip. They ended in a blunt line, not in points like I would have assumed.

I'd completely forgotten the patient until I found a roughly made shiv at my throat. I froze.

"You see? You see?" the patient muttered, his other hand rising to point at the painting.

I could see his hand was coated with tacky blood. His wrist had been gashed open. He pulled me to the open door.

"I need to leave. I am needed. I must spread the word."

We stepped into the light and I saw Alison standing next to a security guard.

Her mouth was agape as she stared at us. I wanted to say something, scream even, but I was frozen, my lips felt numb. I felt my knees begin to shake and suddenly I knew I was going to faint and that, when I did, the knife would slice my throat as I fell against it.

My chest seized up, caught in the tight bands of panic that threatened to take control. I clenched my fists and allowed my nails to bite into the skin, hoping the pain would clear my head. Alison was speaking, trying to calm the patient. I felt him shake his head behind me.

"I must leave. I must. Open the doors. Open them. I need to leave. I am needed. Look and see!" he pointed into his room.

The security guard took a step forward. The patient screamed, grabbing my hair and pulling my head back and exposing my throat.

"No, no, no, no, no!" he screamed.

I saw the hand with the blade rise and I tried to bring my hands up to stop him but they moved so slow, as though in a dream. The patient jerked against me and his hand fell away from my hair as he slumped to the ground. I looked over my shoulder and saw another security guard with a gun raised. I hadn't even heard the shot.

I stumbled away from him and leaned against the wall, trying to catch my breath. My ears rang. I watched Alison kneel next to the man and check for a pulse. She shook her head and a security guard radioed the information back downstairs.

Soon, I was heading down myself. Ellen waited for me in her office. I sat down before her and took the tea she offered. It was Ellen's method. She wanted to be liked by everyone on the staff but she couldn't help being the controlling bitch that she was. So, she made me this tea to seem like she cared that I had almost had my throat cut by some psycho but I could tell by the deep lines around her eyes that she was more angry than concerned.

"I'm glad you're alright," she lied.

I nodded and waited for the axe to drop.

"I can understand that you were concerned for the patient, which made you enter that room without waiting for security. However, now a patient is dead. We have rules for a reason."

I nodded again, staring into the steaming mug.

"Normally, I would put you on an unpaid suspension but we're short-staffed as is. I'll just have to give you a written warning and put this incident in your file. I hope you will learn from this. You've gotten sloppy and I can't have patients dying because of your lack of due diligence," Ellen cleared her throat and stood. "Of course, I am glad you are okay. You may go."

By the time I'd returned to the fifth floor, a janitor had cleaned the blood off the walls and floor. Alison was waiting in tense silence at the nurse's station. I was glad when day broke and the shift ended. Listening to those people scream and cry and whisper all night made me feel like I'd be locked up next.

Walking home, I saw more graffiti. It was everywhere, as if an army of madmen had swamped the city armed with spray paint. I saw shop owners scraping the words off their windows with fast, angry movements, a business man throwing a fit over his vandalized Mercedes that now had a new mouth painted on the hood. I saw the words in chalk on the sidewalk, in paint on walls, and written with marker on the sides of buses. I was glad to finally get home.

My fiancé, Rob, had already left for work. I checked the fridge to see if he'd left me any notes but found none. I showered. Even after scrubbing and scrubbing, I could still feel the patient's hand in my hair and his homemade knife at my throat but I couldn't remember his name. I was too awake to even try falling asleep so I turned on the TV, hoping the sound would make me feel safe again.

I was in an endless black field. Or, maybe it was an ocean. It churned and rose and fell. But it wasn't an ocean and it wasn't a field. It was something awful and I didn't want to see what it was. It was massive, it went on forever, and it was all around me. I didn't want to see, I didn't want to but I couldn't close my eyes to it. I felt it closing in all around me and I opened my mouth to scream.

I woke with a violent start and found the TV blaring fake applause as a contestant correctly guessed an answer. I pulled myself up into a sitting position and checked the time. It was just past six. A voicemail waited for me on my cell. It was Rob, telling me he was going to be late.

I shivered and looked out over the back of the couch. The apartment was dark and empty. I went to the kitchen, turning on all the lights as I went. I double checked my work schedule on the fridge and was relieved to see that I was off for the next two days.

A heavy feeling of sadness hung over me, whether from the incident with the patient or from that fast fading dream I'd had, I couldn't tell. I didn't want to be alone. I tried calling Rob to see when he would be home but only got his voicemail. I tried calling a few friends and when none picked up, I felt this certain knowledge that everyone in the world must have disappeared while I slept. Disappeared into that vast darkness. I clutched at the counter, overwhelmed with that sudden wave of irrational panic.

The sharp, shrill jangle of my phone caused me to scream with fright even as I grabbed it in relief. It was Rob calling me back.

"Sorry babe, I know I'm running late. The CIO, CEO, and a bunch of managers didn't come into work today and no one can seem to get a hold of them. It's been chaos here. I'm just leaving now, let's meet at The Cookery tonight, my treat, huh?"

I wanted to ask him to come get me. That I was too shaken to walk to the restaurant three blocks away but I held it in and just said yes. I got dressed and pulled on my jacket. Through the apartment walls, I could hear the TV of my neighbours. It felt like, with Rob's call, the world and all its cacophony had come back again.

Wrapping my scarf around my neck, I left my apartment building and turned down the dim street. All around me, the words stood out in sickly yellow paint.

Despite being a Friday night, the sidewalks weren't filled with people going to bars or restaurants or clubs as they usually were. The men and women I did see walked at a quick pace—almost a jog—clutching their purses or scarves tight as they rushed to get wherever they were going. Most kept their faces turned down to the ground beneath their feet but others were like me and stared at the words that marked almost every surface.

I heard the crisp crinkle of paper under my feet and looked down. I'd trampled a pamphlet. As I stepped off it, I stopped. Looking up at me in neat black ink was the mouth. Numb, I reached down and picked it up. In a simple font, GODMOUTH was printed across the top in capital letters. Then, underneath, was a detailed drawing of the mouth. Now I could see that what I had thought were teeth were really thick segmented tentacles that draped down from the spherical mouth.

I opened the pamphlet, hoping for an explanation but found only nonsensical gibberish. Over and over the words were printed, sometimes in capitals, sometimes in lower case. Spread throughout were sentences like GRANT US PEACE, RELEASE US, CLEANSE, PURIFY, ERASE, and WE ARE ALL EQUAL INSIDE.

I looked on the back for a printer's logo and found only blank paper. I let the pamphlet drop and wiped my hand on my pants. I continued on my way and saw that the sidewalk was littered with those pamphlets for blocks.

I walked by an open alleyway and heard wailing laughter. I paused and looked in. Five young men and a woman stood in a circle around another woman who was kneeling in the refuse before them. It looked like they were carving something into her forehead with a small pocket knife. The woman looked up at me, said something to the others, and they all turned.

I could see what they had carved into the woman's forehead clearly now because they had already done it to themselves. It was a rough copy of the mouth, standing out crimson with their blood. The woman with the freshly gashed brand smiled as the blood ran down her face. The men leered and began to walk toward me. I turned and ran. Their laughter chased me.

I didn't stop until I was inside The Cookery. Rob was waiting at a table next to one of the front windows. I sat in one of the wicker chairs, the pristine tablecloth rustling against my legs. A tea candle in a pink glass holder flickered between us.

"Hey, sweetie," he reached over and clasped my hand in his. I looked down at my hand in his as I tried to catch my breath.

"Hey, are you alright?" he made as though to stand but I waved him down again.

In short, choppy sentences, I told him what had happened in the alley on the way here. His face went ashen.

"Jesus, I'm so sorry. I should have picked you up, especially with what has been going on lately."

I looked at him and he must have seen the confusion in my face.

"It's been all over the news. They think there's some new gang or something. It's so strange though. I mean, normally gangs tend to stick to an age range or nationality but the members of this gang range from all over."

The waiter walked over and Rob ordered for the both of us. We only ever got the same thing each time we came here; the Konnichiwa Hotdog with wasabi mayo, all beef sausage, bacon, tempura bits, and mayo for Rob and the Bishop Burger with bacon, cheese, panko crusted fried shrimp, the secret sauce, lettuce, and extra pickles for me. Both came with the house special sweet potato fries fried in duck fat. It was all sinfully delicious.

"I haven't heard anything about that," I said, picking at my napkin and tearing bits and pieces off of it.

"I'm not surprised, you never pick up a newspaper and you sleep through the news," Rob laughed.

"Tell me about it then." I wanted to hear him say the word. I wanted to see if it was haunting him like it was me.

"I don't know. They just suddenly appeared, I guess. They don't seem to be involved in drugs or any illegal activity really, besides the fact that they are vandalizing everything they can. One of them got my boss's car two days ago, he was pissed," Rob laughed.

"What—what are they writing?"

Rob shrugged and leaned back as the server brought over our beers, placing them on the table with two solid *thunks*.

"I don't know, the name of their gang or something. Me and the guys think they're some sort of cult like Marilyn Manson's group or whatever."

"Charles Manson," I muttered.

"What?"

I shrugged. I was disappointed. How could he forget that word? Didn't it haunt him too?

GODMOUTH

"A cult makes more sense really. Especially what you said about those fucking kids cutting into their foreheads."

I nodded and looked out onto the street. It was empty now. The twilight was growing thicker, darker. One by one, streetlights flashed on, flooding the street with weak yellow light. One illuminated a mouth drawn on the shop window of a boutique across the street.

"There's no one out tonight," I said.

"What?" Rob looked out, absently, his eyes glazed over in thought, "Oh, they're probably out on Deusore Street or something."

"I doubt it. I think all the sane ones are locked up safely in their homes, hoping to wait out whatever is on its way."

We were both surprised at what I'd said. Rob looked at me long and hard with a worried glint in his eyes. I tried to smile, try to make it seem all like a little joke. Then the server brought us our food, steaming on white porcelain plates and looking like heaven. It gave us an excuse not to talk.

Sunday was bright and beautiful. It was usually the only day we both had off since I normally worked Saturdays. As a treat, Rob had ordered a gourmet picnic from some little shop on Deusore Street and we went to Warden Row Park for lunch. Even though the day was unseasonably warm and the birds sang in the branches above our heads, I felt ill-at-ease.

Rob was as oblivious as ever, in fact, he was even happy. He was convinced that the missing managers meant he'd be getting a promotion soon. He'd hated the missing CIO most of all since he worked directly underneath him. For Rob, everything was looking up.

But I'd seen the people hidden in the alleys, hunched over distinct pamphlets. I'd seen that word everywhere. It crowded out shop windows and blanketed walls, sidewalks, cars. The mouth gaped on stop signs and benches. The city was being swamped. Even the park was not untouched. I'd seen it on the beautiful fountain, the ugly word smeared on it like yellowed feces. Looking at it made me feel dizzy.

"I think I have a good chance at it," Rob was saying, smiling.

"Hey, look at the fountain. Do you see that?" I pointed.

His brow furrowed. He turned and I watched the back of his head. I watched the wind caress his curls.

"I don't know, it's some graffiti," he turned back, shrugging.

"Yeah, but what does it say? I'm curious," I lied.

He glanced over his shoulder for a moment and then picked through the basket to grab another croissant.

"Who cares? Some shithead wrote something dumb."

I stared past him. I could clearly read it.

GODMOUTH

It screamed at me from across the grass.

"Don't you think, honey?" Rob asked and I nodded with a smile.

The day seemed to darken. I looked up into the sky, squinting against the stark daylight. There were no clouds but still there seemed to be a looming darkness that hovered over the city. And yet the sun still shone as if it wasn't there.

"More cheese?"

I shook my head.

Suddenly, I knew we were being watched. I jerked my head and stared back over my shoulder. A woman turned away and bent down to pick up her dog's crap. Beyond her, a man sat on a bench reading the newspaper. I turned my head back and looked beyond Rob. A couple walked by, holding hands. A mother pushed a stroller.

"Hey! Hey!" Rob snapped his fingers in front of my eyes.

I looked at him.

"Jesus, where are you today?"

"Sorry, I guess I thought I heard something."

He studied me. I was relieved when his phone rang. I knew I would have to tell him about the word, about my experience with the dead woman, and the crazed patient. I'd point out the graffiti, the gaping mouth, the pamphlets that littered the streets. But would he think I was crazy?

Rob hung up and grinned.

"They want me in on Monday to talk about the position. I told you, I told you I was next up!"

I smiled along with him. We walked home together holding hands and I watched as he carefully stepped over the pamphlets without really realizing he was doing it. We walked past a dozen or so fresh graffiti marks. I didn't point them out.

After we made love, I dreamed of that dark expanse that wanted to devour me.

I looked all around me and heard others but could not see them. I called out Rob's name but did not hear him. It was closing in. Those dark, moist folds of darkness would wrap around me, and then what?

I woke as Rob pushed himself out of bed, turning off his obnoxious alarm. I felt fuzzy, things seemed out of focus. I tried to go back to sleep as he showered but couldn't.

"Wish me luck, babe," Rob tightened his tie and grinned.

I did so and watched him leave. I spent the day on the couch, watching TV. Normally, I used my days to visit shops, cafes, wherever I wanted but I saw that the streets were still empty this morning as they had been over the weekend. I didn't want to go out there into the silence. I imagined how oppressing the silence would be, how unnerving the emptiness. I thought of the group of kids in the alley, carving simplistic gaping mouths into their foreheads and shuddered.

So, I watched the news instead.

"Police sergeant Roger Morris finally gave a statement regarding this new gang that some citizens have dubbed 'The Mouthers,'" the pretty petite newscaster chirped.

The camera cut to an overweight, graying man in uniform leaning with a weary heaviness against a desk littered with crushed Styrofoam cups, coffee rings, and scattered papers. A crowd of reporters crowded him, microphones jabbing at his face.

"All I have to say is that the situation is being handled. This is not a serious issue."

"What about the recent triple homicide? Weren't the victims brutalized with the image of the mouth carved into their chests?" a reporter shouted over the others.

"Can you comment on the recent massive amount of disappearances in the city?" another reporter pushed forward.

The sergeant wiped his face and slumped further down against the desk.

"All I can say at this time is that the disappearances have not been exclusively linked to any particular event or group."

"What about the murders? Isn't it true the homicide rate is on the rise?"

"I have no other comment at this time except to advise the citizens of this city to stay indoors after dark, keep their windows and doors locked, and to avoid any situation that might place them in danger."

The sergeant turned and waved away the bustling reporters that tried to surge after him. The camera cut back to the perky blonde.

"While the authorities won't confirm that the disappearances that have been on the rise are related to the recent cultish gang activity, I think it's safe to say that there must be some connection. Now, on to Jake with the weather."

I switched it then and let a talk show host scream about the wonders of the new diet pill she had discovered while I waited to go to work. Rob messaged me once, confirming that he'd gotten the promotion. I had to wonder if it was any sort of an accomplishment to get promoted just because your boss had disappeared. *Probably running around naked with a mouth cut into his forehead*, I thought to myself and shuddered.

I didn't relish the idea of walking to work in the empty streets as the sky dimmed but there were also no taxis in sight. I clutched my pepper spray in one hand and avoided all alley entrances, refusing to even look at them.

I arrived twenty minutes early, having practically ran the last block after someone, somewhere started shrieking. Ellen sat behind the desk, her face buried in her hands. The waiting room was as empty and as quiet as the streets.

"Ellen?"

The older woman jumped and looked up with eyes surrounded by the smear of old mascara.

"Oh, it's you. Why did you bother coming in? There's no one here," her lip began to tremble and I was shocked to see the glisten of fresh tears in her eyes.

Ellen was like iron, I'd never seen her scream or yell or cry.

"Ellen?"

I reached out and touched her hand. Maybe she saw this as permission to be weak because she grabbed my hand and pressed her damp face against it, crying. I let her go on for a bit before pulling away. I circled around the desk and put my arm around her.

"What happened, Ellen? Where is everyone?"

She hiccupped and rallied, trying to put on the same mask she wore every day for her staff.

"Dead," she said and shrugged, "or insane. This whole city seems to be going to shit."

Her lip trembled again and she bit it, drawing blood, "My—my Kevin. He went over, he lost it."

Her whole body began to shake and I pressed her tightly against me, trying to quell it.

"He brought home one of those ugly pamphlets. He kept saying how this was the solution everyone needed but didn't know they needed. Then he just left. He didn't even pack his bags. He was just gone. He left his cell phone, his wallet, all his money, and—and—" She stuck out a hand and opened it.

A man's wedding ring glinted in the overhead fluorescent light. We both looked at it. The silence was heavy.

"Where are the other nurses, Ellen? Where are the patients?"

"Gone, I told you. Dead or . . . worse. Yesterday, when the sky went dark in the afternoon, everything went crazy."

I thought about my picnic and the sun that struggled to shine through a dark mass that wasn't there and yet, all the same, hovered over the entire city like a brief storm.

"Beth was killed," Ellen mumbled, "she tried to stop all the psych patients from leaving. You know how she is, always sticking her nose in and meddling. The patient from room 204, Sandy Mitchell, she stabbed Beth in the eye with a pen. I don't even know where she got it from."

I was afraid to ask.

"And Alison?"

Ellen shook her head.

"Alison never showed. She didn't answer her phone either. She's missed two shifts."

"Let's go, Ellen. You should go home."

"I can't," the woman broke down again, "It's so empty there and I keep thinking he's going to come back, but he doesn't and I'm so afraid."

So, I left her there in the empty hospital. The sun had fully set by then and some people were out. It was still so quiet. I pulled my pepper spray out of my purse again and made my way down the sidewalk. Several people had dried blood on their faces and clotted messes on their foreheads, where I assumed they'd carved mouths. Their eyes were raised to the sky; they smiled as if waiting for a great surprise. Others were like me, scared and twitchy.

Rob was on the couch, beer in hand, and watching TV when I stepped in.

"I thought you were at work," he said by way of a greeting.

"No one was there except Ellen. All the patients and staff were gone."

I felt numb, like I was walking through a dream and trying to figure out how to wake up.

"Yeah, we had a skeleton crew going on today too. It was exhausting having to deal with everything."

"The city is going insane."

He looked over at me, his eyes lit up by the light of the TV screen.

"Why do you say that?"

"Are you blind? Don't you see the people walking around with mouths carved into their foreheads? Haven't you seen the pamphlets? The graffiti? It's—it's—" I struggled to say it but couldn't.

I tumbled helplessly to the couch beside him.

"Jesus, hon. You're starting to sound a little crazy yourself."

"You can't not see it! It's everywhere!"

He just looked at me, concern and even a little fear on his face. We sat side by side on the couch, an old Western playing while he nursed a beer and I tried to figure out if I was, in fact, going a little crazy. Beyond the tinny sounds of the movie, I felt the overwhelming and horrible silence of the city. It lay in wait for the pauses between words to creep forward like a living thing.

Later, after we'd brushed our teeth and Rob lay beside me, snoring, I listened for the silence between his breaths. I forced my clenched jaw to relax for the fifth time and forced my fists to open. I looked over and gazed out through the window. All the windows of the neighbouring building were dark. The air felt heavy, pressing down in me.

I thought of the dead woman who spoke the word into my life the very first time. She'd stared up into the sky with a smile on her face. I passed the time until I felt asleep in my memories. It felt safest there. Then I dreamed of nothing but darkness.

In the morning, I felt calm. I stood on our apartment balcony and leaned over the railing. Below I saw that the streets were full of people; it almost looked like a regular workday. Except that most of the people weren't rushing to get to work. Most of the people were standing on the sidewalk or in the street, looking up to the cloudless sky. Most people were waiting.

Rob came up behind me, frowning as he stared down at his phone. I noticed a glaring yellow mouth had been painted across the side of the apartment building across the street. I wondered if I just hadn't noticed it yesterday or if someone had managed to do it just last night in the darkness.

"I got an email from work, they sent out a company-wide mass email. They told us not to bother coming in today."

"Makes sense."

He looked at me. I saw the fear in his eyes. He thought I was losing it but I wasn't. I shrugged and took his hand. I pulled him close against me and looked up. He looked up. It began.

It started slow. The sky began to darken for no reason. If you weren't expecting, you never would have noticed—not at first anyway. Then a great void yawned open, made up of coils of inky darkness, much like smoke. It stretched and stretched until it hung over the whole city. I heard the people on the street below gasp. The darkness became more solid, became more real. In the void, I saw the great, convulsing folds take form. The darkness roiled with fearsome life.

Then four massive, thick tentacles emerged. They were segmented like that of a worm and were of a dusky, dark purplish colour that reminded me of a deep and old bruise. At the tips, the tentacles ended in a multitude of smaller, more flexible appendages that reached and twisted. The massive tentacles moved with a delicate and slow determination. I watched them stretch past buildings until I lost sight of the tips. I felt the impact though. Everyone did. Rob screamed and clutched at me, gripping the balcony railing with his other hand.

"It's an earthquake!" he cried.

He tried to pull me into the apartment but I shrugged him off. I finally realized. Rob couldn't see it. He thought it was an earthquake because he couldn't see the Godmouth. He was blind. He pulled at my arm once before I jerked it away from him. I turned my back on him and stared up at the darkness. Car alarms blared, people screamed in the streets. I heard the apartment's front door slam shut.

I looked down and watched as Rob ran into the street, pushing those who stood still and calm, staring up. The tentacles strained. Their thick flesh bulged with the effort. Then Godmouth began to move. It began to pull itself down. The sun was gone, a false twilight fell upon the city. I felt that I should be afraid but was not. Below, the streets surged with those who were blind to the vast entity that bore down on our city. The drivers drove with desperate frenzy, crashing into those who stood waiting and those others who also tried in vain to escape. The great lips widened, stretched around to encompass the entire city.

There was no escape. I turned and walked out of my apartment, but I did not descend the stairs as Rob had. Instead, I went to the roof. The roof door was unlocked, as always. I saw a few others from the building leaning against the railing, not talking or crying, just watching. I joined them. It was nice to be with people who understood.

Together, we watched Godmouth draw itself ever nearer. I felt the draw of the terrible emptiness between the black folds in the mouth. There was a place for me there. There was a place for all of us there and we would all be made equal. The man standing next to me took my hand. I did not look at him but I was grateful. My hand was cold, his was cold.

The great lips connected with the earth. The city was now trapped beneath the dome that was Godmouth. No escape. All one could do now was wait. But that was alright. I was alright. In the end, it came quickly. A horrible heaviness came first, a crushing weight, pressing down with intent. Then the unnatural silence of a whole city frozen in anticipation. Those massive creeping, undulating folds came down upon us.

They opened and at that moment, looking up at what awaited me, my numbness finally broke and I screamed.

P.L. McMillan is a Canadian expat living in the States, after having taught English for three years in Asia. She is a victim of a deep infatuation with the works of H.P. Lovecraft, Stephen King, and Algernon Blackwood. To her, every shadow is an entry way to a deeper look into the black heart of the world and every night she rides with the mocking and friendly ghouls on the night-wind, bringing back dark stories to share with those brave enough to read them. Some of these chilling stories have been published before with *Neat Magazine*, *Fundead Publications*, and *Sanitarium*.

THE BLACK DOG

by Max D. Stanton

Clay Lachriman was alone in his house except for his dog, and he wasn't entirely sure that the dog was real. It was a bony, foul-smelling little animal of no recognizable breed, with beady rodent eyes and matted, coal-black fur as thick as wire. Clay didn't know how old it was. Sometimes it felt like the dog had been with him since the earliest days of his childhood, even though he was now pushing 40.

The creature sat on the couch next to Clay, watching him keenly as he watched TV. It never barked or snarled, but the noises that it did make were intolerable.

"You're always going to be alone," the black dog said. Its voice was sweet and deep and rich and foul, like a jar of poisoned honey. "Nobody will ever love you."

By force of habit, Clay reached over and scratched the mutt behind its ear. It nuzzled its stinking body up against his and wagged its tail happily.

Every day of Clay's life was more or less the same, and it was a bad day. An alarm dragged him out of a fitful sleep full of half-remembered nightmares. He performed his daily toilet, and choked down pills that were supposed to make thinking tolerable. He drove a grueling commute to a remote office park, where he processed paperwork on behalf of a vast international conglomerate. In the evening, he returned to his flimsy home in a cheap sub-development to sit before glowing rectangles, and occasionally masturbate. Periodic notices arrived in the mail, informing him of the size of his debt. Clay wholly expected this pattern to continue for the rest of his life.

There were few other Lachrimans remaining. Both of his parents were dead and he had only one sibling, a sister, with whom he shared almost nothing in common besides predisposition to a few genetic diseases. There was possibly an uncle in Chicago, but maybe not. Clay hadn't seen him for decades. Clay had known a good bunch of friends once, but over time they had drifted out of touch or moved to faraway cities or were otherwise lost to him. Social media was a poor replacement. Seeing his old companions' pets and children and vacations from afar brought him no joy.

As the people Clay loved exited his life one by one, the black dog stepped up to fill the void they left behind. No other person seemed to notice the canine's presence, although animals went berserk when they saw it. At work the dog settled in under his desk and dozed contentedly as he labored, sometimes whispering to him that his life was a meaningless failure. On the rare occasions when he went out on the town, it trotted unleashed by his ankles, offering its running commentary. Somehow it all seemed completely natural to Clay. He did wonder, once in a while, if he had gone insane.

One Saturday, Clay overcame his torpor long enough to get out to a museum. He was inspecting some important French paintings of flowers when the dog presented its critique. "It's funny to think that the frog who painted these dumb-looking tulips has been dead for centuries, but people still remember his name," it said. "You, on the other hand—nobody knows who you are even though you're still walking around. Why do you think that is?" The animal raised one of its rear legs and sprayed hot piss onto the marble wall.

"Let's just move on," Clay said. "I don't like still-lifes that much, anyway."

In the next gallery, a nude of a fleshy, rosy-cheeked wood nymph captured Clay's interest. "Boy, I'll bet the guy who painted this was balling his models bow-legged," said the dog. "None of that for you, though. Like the sign on the wall says, you can look, but you don't get to touch."

Clay couldn't stand to look at the paintings any more. He gazed over at an attractive, prosperous-looking couple of about his own age that was walking the gallery hand-in-hand. The man had a pink-faced, cooing infant strapped to his chest in some sort of yuppie papoose.

"Go home," the dog said. "You don't belong here and everyone knows it. The good people can't enjoy themselves while a morlock like you is skulking around."

"Yeah, this isn't my scene," Clay said, and he packed it in early though he'd visited barely half of the galleries and hadn't even made it to the special Egyptian exhibit he'd paid extra to see. Ventures to sporting events, restaurants, nature trails, and Christian worship were cut short in similar fashion.

With the black dog by his side, looking at beautiful things stung Clay with painful longing, and so he came to look at ugly things exclusively. Being around other people only heightened his sensation of loneliness, and so he embraced solitude.

Clay did not feed the black dog wet food or kibble or even table scraps but nonetheless, it thrived, gradually growing from the size of a toy poodle or large rat to about the dimensions of a cocker spaniel. Clay grew much larger as well, but not because he was thriving.

Once Clay had been a reasonably tidy man, but dealing with the dog sapped his energy to the point where he began letting his dirty dishes and soiled clothes and garbage lie wherever they came to rest. His toilet broke but he could not bear to have a plumber see how grimy and seedy his home was, so he delayed calling one and implemented workaround solutions with plastic milk jugs that made the griminess and seediness so much worse.

One day the black dog urged Clay to cover up all of the windows so that no sunlight could enter the house, and to draw strange symbols and formulae on the interior walls and ceilings with a black magic marker. Clay did not see the point of decorating his home with six-pointed stars and runes he could not read, but while he worked on this errand the black dog was blessedly silent. It had been so long since Clay had possessed the wherewithal for any sort of big project that the mere sensation of doing something was a pleasing novelty, even though the task itself was dubious and sinister.

Clay sat on his couch surrounded by empty or half-empty fast food wrappers, smoking a cigarette and ashing into a bowl with dried soup still sticking to its rim. The black dog lay across his lap, contentedly licking at its master's thighs. It was midday but with the windows sealed up they were in near-total darkness, illuminated only by the pale glow of the television set.

Clay's TV had been acting strangely ever since he had decorated his walls. Its sides had gone soft, the grey plastic taking on a texture not unlike flesh, and it had begun picking up channels that he had never subscribed to. On the other hand, the picture quality was still fine so he didn't see any reason to replace it.

An episode of the Brady Bunch was playing, a Thanksgiving episode. Onscreen, the eponymous bunch sat for the feast, the boys dressed as Indians and the girls as pilgrim women. The Brady boys were naked but for breechcloths and moccasins of uncured leather, with gaudy white and crimson war paint applied in wild spirals. They were each bedecked with garlands of ears and scalps, and Bobby wore an elaborate necklace beaded with human teeth. The girls' costumes were plainer, more recognizable as holiday-special fare, but for the scarlet 'A' on Marsha's breast.

At the head of the table, Father Brady clutched a vicious-looking obsidian blade in one hand and a long fork in the other, and croaked out a benediction in some queer, pre-Columbian tongue, heavy on the glottal sounds and consonants, and interspersed with incongruous snippets of Latin. It was all incomprehensible to Clay but evidently there were punchlines in there somewhere judging from the gleeful reaction shots of the Brady brood and the harsh, insistent, hyena-like braying of the laugh track. Occasionally Clay found himself chuckling mirthlessly along with the canned laughter despite the language barrier.

"I don't believe that I've seen this episode before," said Clay.

"Shut up, dummy, I'm watching this," replied the dog.

Onscreen, Alice wheeled out a cart with Jan hog-tied atop it. "Hope you all like white meat!" she cheerfully announced. Then it was all shrieks and tearing. Clay looked morosely at the Brady blood feast on his television screen, and at the wretched canine sitting on him, and something within him shifted. He pushed the dog off of his lap. When it resumed its position, he pushed it away more forcefully.

"Hey, screw you!" the dog snarled. "I was sitting there."

"Go to hell," Clay said. "I have taken enough of your shit, and it has not done me any good at all. You are a bad dog."

"What, you think you ought to have the best in show? We get what we deserve in life. That's why you've got me."

"I'm not going to listen to you anymore. Name one man of distinction who got ahead in life by listening to what his dog told him. Son of Sam doesn't count. Your kind goes about in public naked and leashed, pissing on lampposts. Your counsel is not to be trusted."

"So, what are you going to do about it?" the dog asked, baring its teeth.

"I'm going out for a walk," Clay said. "And I'm leaving you behind."

It was a sunny day with a brisk, pleasant breeze, ideal for directionless strolling. The black dog slunk after

Clay growling insults at its master, but it kept a longer distance than usual. "Don't kid yourself, a walk in the park doesn't change anything," the dog said. "You'll never be happy."

"Of course, I won't be happy, if I sit around feeling sorry for myself and watching fucked-up TV all day. What I'm doing isn't working, so I need to make a change."

"Change takes strength, you feeble little bitch, and you don't have any. Clay, listen to me. You are well beyond redemption by now."

"That's not fair. I know I'm not the best guy in the world, but I'm not so bad. The worst things that I do are eating too much crap and watching too much television, and last I checked those weren't hanging crimes. People have done worse. I've got to stop being so hard on myself." He took a deep breath and enjoyed the feel of the wind on his skin. The dog fell silent and stayed that way for the rest of the walk.

Clay began jogging and lifting weights at the gym, and while he didn't stick with the program as closely as he'd hoped he would, neither did he accept the black dog's repeated invitations to abandon exercise entirely. A few pounds dropped off of his doughy frame, and his energy started to return. He made conscious efforts to care for himself, and even sought out the companionship of the opposite sex. For a while his experiences in online dating provided incredibly rich material for the dog to abuse him with, but then his co-worker Liz from two cubicles over set him up with a friend of hers named Kathy.

Kathy was a recently separated woman, slightly older than Clay, who worked as a school administrator and adored dolphins and show tunes. On first impression, she was not a great beauty, but a closer look revealed that she had lovely grey eyes and delicate hands that could have gotten her a career as a glove model. Most importantly, she was wonderful company. In her presence, Clay did not feel ashamed.

Clay never invited her to his home, of course, and was haunted by a terror that she would learn how he lived and leave him. But the terror was useful since rather than paralyzing him as fear usually did, it drove him to start the long-delayed process of cleaning the place up. Sometimes Clay looked at the eldritch graffiti all over his walls and wondered what he had been thinking when he put it there. He decided to have it painted over.

Meanwhile, the black dog was sick. It looked like one of the traumatized pups from humane society ads, with its ribs clearly defined and its skin rotten with mange, except that even in its infirmity, nothing about it evoked the slightest pity. On some days, especially when Clay had a date planned with Kathy, the filthy animal slipped away to a secret place where Clay could not see it or hear it.

One night after chain-restaurant Mexican food and a particularly heroic intake of margaritas, Kathy took Clay back to her place. The sex was fumbling and tender and sweet. Clay's manhood had grown so used to the caresses of Madam Palm and her five ugly daughters that it barely remembered what to do with an actual woman, but it acquitted itself well enough regardless. Afterwards Clay lay in the dark enjoying the feel of Kathy's head resting on his chest, and the adorable, whistling sound of her snores, and the smell of mingled sweat and perfume, and he wondered if his dog was finally dead.

Then he heard the clicking of its nails and he saw the animal crouched in the corner of Kathy's bedroom, licking at its sores. "It'll never last," the dog said.

The dog was proven right a week later. Kathy sent Clay a text saying that she was getting back together with her ex; that Clay was a nice guy but that he needed to work on his issues. Clay called Kathy and said some harsh things in reply. He called back five minutes later with intent to apologize, but by then she'd already blocked his number.

When Clay got back to his house, the black dog was waiting for him on the stoop with a beaming canine smile, as fat and sleek as it had ever been. The dog leapt onto him just as he began to cry and licked the tears from his cheeks with its slimy, sandpaper tongue.

"Your mistake was letting that dirty bastard Hope get a shot at you," the dog said. "Hope is just the herald and harbinger of despair. Nothing more. But it's all right, buddy, you've always got me." Clay threw his arms around the creature's neck and wept freely. After that he never doubted the dog again.

Clay fell into a melancholy stupor that made his previous ruts look like triumphs by comparison. On many days, he didn't have the energy to do anything but lie in bed, chain-smoke, and stare up at the cryptic marks he'd drawn on his ceiling, while his dog nuzzled up close under his arm and whispered imprecations into his ear. Eventually he was fired from his job, and then he barely had to leave the house at all. His unemployment swelled the black dog to the size of a Great Dane.

Squalor reclaimed all the places that Clay had cleaned, and salted the Earth. Columns of ants infested his kitchen counters and trash-strewn rooms, and flies buzzed thick in the air. Clay took to carrying a can of aerosol poison. When insects crawled on his bare skin, he sprayed them with death, but like a callous World War I general, the ant queen kept sending wave after wave of her soldiers to die pointlessly in the gas. The poison added a new tang to the already-overpowering miasma. Clay's skin erupted in furious red rashes, and the chemical stench gave him a headache that never went away, but he figured that he could bear those symptoms better than he could bear the bugs climbing all over him.

One day, Clay was curled up on the floor stroking his dog's fur and quietly weeping when he felt tell-tale tickles on the hairs of his calf. He sprayed his leg with poison, and then brushed the tiny corpses away. Moments later, however, the ants started moving again. He gave them another long blast of the gas, until the ground beneath them was damp, but they continued to march. Clay swatted them with his palm, crushing them . . . and yet they did not stop. Another ant came over to investigate. One of her smashed sisters bit her head off.

Clay got to his feet—no little undertaking, given his girth—and pushed back his couch with a strained gasp to reveal the cockroaches that he knew lived beneath it. He crushed one of the vermin beneath his bare heel with an audible *crunch*, pressing its entrails into a carpet already so dirty that a deposit of roach guts barely made a difference anymore. The insect did not stop wiggling. Its top half crawled in one direction still dangling its insides behind it, and the bottom went the opposite way.

From that point on Clay's house was a zombie apocalypse-writ miniature. The dead hunted the living without mercy, seeking them out in the innumerable nooks and crannies of Clay's heaped garbage. Dead flies fluttered in the light fixtures until they burned to immobile cinders. Dead ants staggered back into their burrows to slaughter the queens who had birthed them. The insecticide stopped having any effect at all. Clay's only option was to crush the bugs when they crawled onto him, and even when he did so their limbs continued to squirm. Eventually he stopped even trying to brush them away.

"Damn, look at this place," the black dog chuckled. By now the dog was wolf-sized, like a beast from a fairy tale. Smoke poured from its nostrils and its panting jaws when it spoke. "You'll never make Good Housekeeping now."

"Oh, I don't know about that," Clay said softly. "Do they run a Halloween issue?"

Clay was woken from a nap by a knock on the front door, a sound that he had not heard in a very long time. He treaded lightly to the entrance, being careful not to disturb any of the piles of garbage in the same manner that one might be careful not to disturb a large, sleeping animal. Kathy was on the other side of the peephole. "Clay?" she asked, knocking again and more insistently. "Clay, I want to talk with you."

Clay undid the bolt but not the chain and opened the door a crack. "How did you find me here?"

"Liz looked you up in your company's directory. Gee, Clay, don't you ever mow your lawn? It looks like a jungle out there."

Clay barely even remembered that he had a lawn. "Oh yeah," he said. "I haven't been feeling good lately. What do you want?"

"Liz told me that you're not doing well. I just wanted to talk with you. I'm not happy with how we left things, and I thought it'd be better if we spoke in person. Can I come in?"

"It'd be better if you didn't."

"Please, Clay, just let me in."

"Let her in," the black dog ordered coldly. Clay's heart froze as he thought about Kathy seeing him in his degraded condition, but his fingers undid the chain.

Clay winced to see Kathy's shock as she stepped over the threshold. She took a handkerchief from her purse and held it over her nose and mouth. "Oh. My. God. Liz told me that you'd been really depressed since we broke up and that you'd lost your job, but I—I had no idea things were this bad for you. This is like something from one of those TV shows. Why did you board up all the windows? And what are these drawings on the walls? Oh my God." She began climbing the stairs to the second floor, tracing the patterns with her pink, glossy fingertip.

"No," Clay said. "Not your god. Not your god at all. It was a dog who did this. You shouldn't be here. I don't think it's safe." He glanced nervously at the black dog. The animal was drooling.

"No, this clearly isn't safe," Kathy said, peering disdainfully at the piss jugs stacked by the bathroom. "This whole house might have to be condemned."

"Condemned. That's a good word for it."

"Lock the door," the black dog said.

Clay resisted this command with every bit of his willpower, but his willpower had long since wasted away to scraps. He turned the deadbolt and put the chain back on. Just then there was an enormous crash from upstairs, like an over-stuffed dumpster vomiting up its contents, followed closely by the sound of something large shambling about.

"What's that?" Kathy asked. "Clay, is anyone else living here?"

"I'm not really sure," Clay said. "I used to think it was just me and my dog, but lately I've been thinking that the garbage hoard itself might be alive. At night, I can hear it breathing through pop-bottle nostrils and plastic bag lungs. I try not to wake it up."

A vast pile of decaying waste slithered into view at the top of the stairs. It was not merely sliding about due to gravity but moving with definite purpose, a hideous new life spontaneously generated from the unbounded wretchedness that Clay existed in. The beast roared wetly, spraying urine and morsels of spoiled food, and then it tumbled down the stairs and absorbed Kathy into its mass as it rolled over her. She had time to scream once before she was swallowed up. There was some thrashing and struggling from inside the pile, and one of Kathy's hands burst free grasping feebly for a lifeline, her manicured nails brown and smeared with waste. Then the pile squeezed in on itself tightly like a heart beating, accompanied by a squeal and the sound of crushing bone, and all was still again. From that day forth, the house's bouquet included the sickly-sweetish smell of rotting human flesh.

The black dog woofed happily, and rolled over for a belly rub.

Eventually the black dog swelled to occupy the entirety of Clay's home. Clay burrowed into its side and nested there like a tick. His whole world was an expanse of hot, oily, abyss-colored fur that heaved gently with each breath the monster took. The two lived as mutual parasites, with Clay sustaining himself by drinking his dog's vile blood, and the dog sustaining itself by drinking its master's despair. Clay's consciousness atrophied until the only thoughts he could think were tick thoughts, dim and ugly and occupied wholly by an incessant need to suckle.

Then one day the black dog vanished.

Clay awoke naked and coated with filth in his septic ruin of a home, dazed and frightened by the sudden absence of the being that had dominated him for so long. Very little of his mind was left, but some intuition told him that he should go outside.

As he opened the door, exposing himself to blistering daylight and fresh air that scorched his throat, Clay became aware of an animalistic roar bubbling up from behind him and a sensation of motion at his legs, like he was standing at the center of a foul and slow-moving river. His hideous hoard poured out of his house in an undulating column, an enormous, baleful serpent made of rotten trash and excrement. It sloshed into the gutters, devouring the muck and imbuing it with its own hideous semblance of life.

Then came the dead swarm. Thousands of deceased insects spilled outside in a pestilential cloud, burrowing into the soil and flying through the air. The sickness in his home was spreading throughout the world to poison the whole of the animal kingdom.

The daylight turned crimson and inky blackness spread across the sun, leaving only a thin tendon of bloody red at the edge. Clay, now far beyond the warnings he'd received in elementary school, stared directly into the eclipse. He saw his own dog staring back at him from the sky, its eyes burning holes in the firmament like incoming meteors.

"I never knew your name," Clay murmured.

"They call me Fenris," said the wolf, in a voice as loud and terrible as atomic war. "I needed something soft to eat before I was strong enough to hunt." One by one the stars went out as the wolf pulled them into its omnivorous maw. Clay sat down on his stoop as the darkness deepened, letting the trash and crawling death wash over him, and watched his black dog swallow the last of the light.

Max D. Stanton is an academic and writer of weird tales who lives in Philadelphia with his great hound Bear and his imperious cat Tristan. You can find his work in publications including *World Unknown Review*, *Sanitarium Magazine*, *Disturbed Digest*, *Lovecraftiana* [forthcoming] and the *Under a Dark Sign* and *Candlesticks & Daggers* anthologies.

DEATH CARRIAGE

By Matthew Penwell

When I arrived in Marywood, nightfall was approaching. Two streetlights with dying flames greeted me. I went down the main street, feeling tired, and needing a good night's rest. I looked for a house that suggested any sort of boarding, but found none. The houses are small, most one story, and have a particular "old" look about them. I have searched my mind for a better word to put on them and have failed to find one.

I passed a side road, going off to my left, and was about to go down it when I spotted a man emerging from his house, wrapping a coat about his shoulders.

"Hallo," I said to the man, approaching him.

He looked up at me in fright, slightly flinching back, his eyes wide and mouth ajar. The man looked as if he had just seen a ghost. His cheeks quickly regained their color. His mouth twisted into a snare.

"What do you want? Why are you riding a horse about town after dark?"

"I'm sorry, sir," I responded, feeling confused. "I'm passing through town, and I was looking for a place to board for the night."

"Brick house, on the corner. Light should be on in window. They *always* have a vacancy." The man's eyes shifted, he looked me up and down, and then gave my horse a good looking over. "Best be on my way."

The man hurried away, down the street.

I found the house readily enough. A two-story, brick, with an overhang over the stoop. Just like the man said, a light was on in the left window. I dismounted my horse and looked for something to secure him to. I noticed a series of hooks fastened into the ground. I lead him closer to the house and tied one end of a rope about his neck, the other about the hook.

I tried the door handle and found it locked. *Odd*, I said to myself. In all my travels, I had never encountered the entrance to a boarding house to be locked—especially if they had a vacancy. I knocked as hard as I could. *Perhaps the owner had fallen asleep*, I thought. I waited; eventually, the door opened.

A man dressed in a nightgown answered. He had a thick mustache of orange and only a few wisps of hair remained on his head. He looked at me, his eyes slits, one hand fishing about in the chest pocket of his gown. He found his glasses and put them on. A candle cast a golden red hue on one side of his face.

"I met a man in town who said you had a vacancy?"

"Fifteen cent a night. Twenty, if you want breakfast in the morning."

I paid the man at the door; he inspected the money as if he thought it to be fake. I had met two men in the small town, and they had both searched me over like I was from another world. My stomach was beginning to feel a little unsettled. The man moved away from the door, letting me pass by. He turned quickly about, closed the door, and locked it.

The living quarters were large. Several book shelves lined the wall to my right, while on my left, a doorway opened up. The man moved past me, towards the kitchen. A wood stove stood in the corner, piles of kindle and logs on either side. A long table with five seats sat in the direct middle of the room. I could make out a small staircase towards the back.

"Go up the stairs. First room on your right. Door is open. If you smoke, open the window. I don't want my house smelling like tobacco."

I went to the stairs and looked up. Without a candle, I felt like I was about to walk into the darkness of death. I went up slowly, the steps creaking and bowing under my weight. On the landing, I saw that all the doors were open but one. I supposed this was the owner's room. A painting of a woman in evening wear hung on the wall beside the door. I could barely see it in the moonlight, but I made out enough to see that the woman was young, black haired, and had a grim sort of smile.

"This one," the man said, behind me. I hadn't heard him walk up the stairs. I rounded quickly, my hands balling into fists, ready for a fight. The man was pointing at the open door on my right. He handed me the candle holder. "There is a pail in the corner if you need to relieve yourself."

I looked at the man. "Does this place not have an outhouse?'

"We do, but it's in your best health to not go outside after dark."

"But why? Did something happen? The man I saw in the streets looked at me like he was seeing a ghost."

I saw the same shift in the owner of the border's house that I had seen in the man's outside. It was an agitated look, one that suggested I shouldn't ask questions, or that I was asking too many questions. The man turned away, removed his glasses from his face, and stuck them back in his pocket. Even before the man uttered the words, I knew the conversation was over.

"Be off to bed. Shall I wake you in the morning?"

"I'll wake on my own. G'night."

The man shuffled down the hall, opened the closed door, and disappeared within. I turned and went into my own room. Looking about, I noticed there was a bed and a two-drawer dresser with a small mirror attached for shaving. Nothing else. I went to the bed and sat atop it. The fresh smell of the blanket and pillow held no reminder that someone else had slept on it. I set the candle on the dresser and went about untying my shoes. I put them beside the bed, hoisted my feet up, and weaved myself under the cover. I blew the candle out.

In spite of my heavy lids, I couldn't fall asleep. I turned onto my side and looked out the window of the room. Through the curtains, a shaft of moonlight shone onto the floor. The world outside was quiet. Being a native of New York, I was used to the sound of horses and carriages at all hours of the night; the shouting of people as they stumbled home from the saloon. I determined that's what it was: it was too quiet. The longer I lay there, the more I thought about the man on the street. Everything about his demeanor suggested he wasn't expecting to meet another person walking about. The sight of myself had nearly frightened him to death.

The picture of the man's fear-stricken face stayed with me. It was there when I closed my eyes: the hollow eyes, the balding head with the wind moving about the last remaining strands of hair, the red beard. The man's face was with me when sleep came, washing over me in a wave of discomfort.

I awoke. The room was dark. The shaft of moonlight had moved away from my window with the rotation of the moon. With my eyes adjusted to the darkness, I could make out the shapes of the room. I threw the cover off me and made my way to the pail in the corner. No matter how hard I tried, my mind couldn't wrap itself around the concept. The man had said they had an outhouse, but insisted I didn't use it—insisted I didn't go outside. Had there been a murder recently? Is that why he didn't want me going outside? I undid the button on my trousers and relieved my bladder. When I finished, I went to the window and looked out. The streetlights had been extinguished during my slumber, leaving the town cloaked in black. I went back to the bed and sat on the edge, still looking out the window.

What time of night, I couldn't tell. I had seen a clock in the foyer upon entering, but decided not to entertain myself by going to check the time. Instead, I checked the drawer for a box of matches. I found one in the bottom drawer, next to a Bible. I took the matches and lit the candle. The hue of the light casted shadows across the room, flickering ghosts. I no longer felt tired. I felt as if I had slept for days. I had it in my mind that I would stay awake until sunbreak, and then continue my travel. I didn't need a meal. There was food on my horse that would sustain me. But I needed something to do in the meantime. I pulled out the bottom drawer, got the Bible, and thumbed through it, reading a passage here and there.

I found the passage about Moses and decided to read the story in its entirety.

I read until I felt tired. My lids were once again heavy. Putting the old book on the nightstand, I blew out the candle, and lay there, listening to the silent air. From somewhere far away, I heard a cough that made my heartrate rise. Sleep was trying to wash over me. I kept dozing in and out. It was during this period that I heard the noise outside.

A carriage, the wooden wheels rolling over the cobblestoned road. I sat up in bed. *Surely my mind is playing tricks on me.* And looked at the window. A chill unlike anything I can describe trailed down my spine. My arms and legs rippled in gooseflesh. The room about me felt like it had dropped several degrees, but on the latter, I can't be sure. I reached for the candle and thought better of it. I didn't want the person thinking someone was prying on their privacy. So, I went to the window, pulled back the curtain an inch, and looked out into the dead street.

There were four of *them*. Not horses, but things that I will try my best to put into words. They were short, tanned skin, like old, worn out, baggy leather. Their ears came to a point below strands of oily hair. Their eyes were black and wide and glowed in the moonlight like onyx orbs. Two knife-like teeth protruded over their bottom lip. They were naked, save for a loincloth tied about their midsection. Each of the four things had a rope in their long-fingered hand, and hung over their back like a man carrying a heavy sack. They stepped in unison, their bare feet not making a sound. My eyes trailed from the things, up the rope, to the carriage. A man held the ropes in his hand, two in each. I couldn't make out much of his features, due to the black cloak he was wearing. But it looked as if he wore a hat under his hood, for it didn't go down his face but stuck out on either side. I noticed his hands. The moonlight made them look gray, like ash. He uttered something in a language that I do not have the faintest knowledge of. The things holding the rope hurried up their speed. The carriage had no roof, and I could see right inside it. A body lay inside, it's arms crossed over its chest, its eyes closed. I could see it was the body of a female by its long hair.

My mind tried to grasp at what I was seeing. The things pulling the carriage weren't human, I know that. My mind drifted off into fantasy. Being somewhat familiar with European folklore, a word came to mind. But I rejected the idea as soon as it came. Goblins were a thing of pure fantasy, made up, impossible to exist. But I had read stories about encounters with the small, squat men with large eyes and pointed ears. *Dreaming. This isn't real.* The carriage made a sudden right, disappearing into the forest line.

I stood at the window for a while longer, shaking, my body feeling like it had been dropped into a frozen pond. I let go of the curtain, letting it fall back into place. My legs felt like rubber. I reached out blindly, found the wall, and braced myself against it, trying to calm myself. Slowly, I made my way to my bed and sat on the edge. I sat there until sunrise. I don't believe I moved until I heard movement outside my door.

I sprang from the bed, ran to the door, and threw it wide. A woman let out a small scream and rounded on me.

"Who are you?" she demanded.

"I came here last night," I told her, trying to keep my voice steady. "A man welcomed me in."

The woman nodded. "Breakfast will be made shortly."

"Ma'am," I said, reaching out for the woman. She turned to face me. I shook my head. "Never mind."

The woman looked at me oddly, turned, and went down the stairs.

I went back in my room and made the bed. Ten minutes later, I heard another pair of footsteps pass my room and go down the stairs. From below me, I heard voices: man, and woman. The woman said something I didn't make out, but I heard the man loud and clear: "No, I told him not to go outside."

When I joined the couple, they were sitting at the table. A bowl of boiled eggs sat in the middle, next to a pan of cornbread. I pulled out five cents from my pocket and paid the man for the meal, sat down. The woman passed me a plate. I put a slab of cornbread and three boiled eggs on it.

"Sir," I said, "what did I see last night? That's the reason you didn't want me to go outside."

The man looked at his wife. She looked back, as if trying to communicate without speaking. I watched their faces. The woman's bottom lip trembled as she brought an egg to her mouth and took half of a bite. The man continued to look at his wife. He refused to make eye contact with me. Finally, he spoke:

"What *did* you see last night?"

The question shocked me. "Well, I don't know, exactly."

"Best to keep it that way, then."

"I saw a carriage," I admitted, "it was being drawn by four men—only, they weren't men. And the carriage had a body in it, a female."

"Bella Gein," the woman said. "That's who you saw."

"Who?"

"She was hanged last night for the murder of her husband," the man said, gravely. "Believed in devilment, witchcraft, lived out in the woods. Thought she could get away with it."

I nodded but didn't say another word. I no longer felt like eating. I said goodbye to the man and woman and thanked them for their courtesy. The man walked me to the door. We stood on the sidewalk together.

"Did they notice you?" the man asked me, his voice low.

"No."

"It's best you leave now and don't talk about it with anyone."

I untied my horse from the hook and straddled it. I started down the road, out of town. When I was a quarter mile away, I looked over my shoulder. The owner of the house had retreated inside. Turning my horse about, I headed towards the area where I thought I had seen the carriage vanish.

As I got closer, all the hair on my arms stood on end. My horse refused to go any farther. I dismounted him and tied him to a tree. I took a few steps into the leaf-covered ground, and looked about. There was no way a carriage could pass through here. The trees were too dense. I walked back out of the forest.

"What you doing?" a boy asked me, running to me, his eyes wide with panic, his feet kicking up dust. "Don't go back there. The caves are back there. That's where the devil lives."

My heart jumped into my throat. I untied the horse as quickly as I could. My fingers felt numb as I picked at the knot. My mind made the calculations. I handed the boy a bill note as I mounted my horse. I had never wanted to get away from a place so much in my life.

Matthew Penwell was born in Florida, spent a majority of his life in a small town in Tennessee, and now currently resides in an even smaller town in Ohio. When he isn't writing or working, Matthew spends most of his time practicing the guitar, listening to Black Metal, and reading. Influences include: Bradbury, Stine, and Faulkner. This is his first publication.

THE LITTLE DEAD THING

by John S. McFarland

Abel Edwin Jarre
128 Constantinople St.
St. Odile

Mr. George M. Nance
441 William St.
Pittsburgh
Nov. 16, 1922, Thursday

George:

If I can't discover how to heal the wound God has put in my heart to know Him, to understand and satisfy my longing for Him and finally feel I am a part of His creation, I don't know how I will face the years to come. I'm sorry to make these ravings (or musings) the main part of my letters lately, and perhaps that is why you have not answered me in so long, but I find I can hardly think about anything else.

You've heard this before, ever since Fismette. Before the war I never questioned that I knew the heart and will of God. I knew God kept me apart and disconnected from the world for some reason which would someday be apparent to me. So arrogant when you think about it, that any of us can understand the will of God! That day in Fismette when the Germans finally crossed the river and that boy, that German soldier of maybe twenty years of age who was carrying the flame thrower canister—remember when the bullet struck the tank and the lad went up in flames, remember how our boys cheered? It was a spectacle, an entertainment. We cheered and laughed as he, the enemy, screamed in the most horrific and pitiful agony. I aimed my rifle at his head to put an end to his suffering, but I hesitated. He was an enemy soldier, yes, but would not the act of shooting him in that way be something other than the accepted barbarity of war? I knew, as the Church says, I would have a murder on my hands, a mercy killing. This boy who may have been raised a Catholic as I was, who only thought he was doing his duty to his country, must die slowly and painfully so that I may not have a mortal sin on my soul. Lieutenant Allen shot him, mercifully, so his immolation only lasted a few seconds.

I killed two men that day, two I know of. Acceptably as a protocol of battle. I shot them on the bridge and they fell into the river. It didn't affect me any more than putting my boots on that morning. They were strangers, objects, targets, the enemy. But that night I could only think of the burned boy who died in such a different way. I wondered how is the suffering and loss of an enemy, the *other*, different from ours? Of course, it isn't. An obvious enough proposition, but I didn't really *understand* it before then. But the war was full of moments like that wasn't it? As we said on the ship home that night when our time in the 111th was nearly over: War is moments where familiar things became understood in a different way, or understood more deeply. It's that connection that must be made to this world, to all of life which I have been seeking and turning over in my head for four years. I'm sorry to refer to it so often. One day I hope to put it out of my mind.

With your wife's serious illness maybe you have had these pointless 'metaphysical' thoughts too? I am glad Mae is feeling better (per your last letter in March), and her consumption was relieved by your trip to Arizona. Perhaps you will move there? I would hope to see you again and to meet her on your way west, if you do. I wish we had been able to do that on your first trip, but there it is.

I write to Eustace Kirby too as you may remember. He was as near as the landing at DeCastres Island in my very town in June, according to the visitor list in the newspaper, and he didn't visit me. "Eustace Kirby of Bremen Ridge, Pennsylvania who served with distinction in the 111th Pennsylvania in the recent war, travelling to San Francisco, California with his wife Kate. The Kirbys came by boat down the Ohio then up the Mississippi to catch the train in Ste. Odile and travel north to their connection in St. Louis to continue their journey." I have written him seven or eight times since getting reestablished here in Ste. Odile. He was a few blocks away and chose not to visit me. I am at a loss to understand this.

I mentioned in my last letter also that my hopes of a future with my Lucy were fading. Her father has never approved of me. She says he wants no veteran of the war for her husband. He suspects that no man who lived through it would be unaffected enough to make a suitable mate for his daughter. He would never thrust such a man to be capable of a normal family life after all we experienced. I have asked her for a final answer, asked that she consider only her own feelings, not her family's. I am still waiting to hear from her.

My work continues at the assay laboratory at Osage Lead Company. Mr. Karl, my supervisor has hired a new technician; Roualt is his name. He is supposed to be my assistant, and I am to train him to process samples. The young man is concerned with details and organization and is good enough at arithmetic, so he is learning quickly, as I expected he would. It seemed to me there were barely enough samples to keep me occupied, as our production has fallen off so drastically since the war, but Karl has insisted that we will be much busier in the future, that there are prosperous times ahead, and we must be prepared. He has said there will soon be a push to add lead to gasoline, as it makes automobile engines run smoother, and our production will soon increase. But, I was unconvinced by this assertion and I asked Karl if he is dissatisfied with my work, or has come to dislike me for some reason, but he says I am imagining it. He says I spend too much time imagining plots against myself. I don't know what it is, George, but the town has not accepted me, since I returned from the army. Treves has noticed it too, noticed that he is ostracized now. In his case his injuries have changed his appearance so terribly; perhaps that is what is behind his situation. His surgery has fallen off to nothing. But as far as I can tell, I am unchanged, outwardly at least. But Ste. Odile has changed toward me. I am an outsider here.

Though I still harbor some concern for him, even Treves seems alien to me. What are the chances that two fellows from a tiny village on the Mississippi should find themselves at the outbreak of a great war, in the same unit in a Pennsylvania battalion? I would have taken no bet on it! You would think with that great coincidence and the unifying experience of what came after, we would be brothers or fast friends thereafter, but we hardly have two words to say to each other. There it is.

I will close now so I do not miss the mailman.

Your Friend,
Abel

Later
November 17, Friday

George:
I dozed off and missed sending yesterday's letter. Much has happened today. My suspicions were correct. Karl dismissed me this morning. He said my work had suffered recently, which I know is not true. He said Roualt can replace me very well now and at a lower rate of pay. And Karl is hiring a friend of Roualt's to be *his* assistant at an even lower rate. There it is! Dismissed! A veteran rewarded for his service. I had few personal things to retrieve, collected my $7.00 in wages and walked the several blocks home to Constantinople Street.

It turned much colder overnight and the wind whipped in from the river as I made my way home. I have saved $42.00 which might sustain me for a few weeks but as I walked against that cold wind I knew I must find other employment quickly, and that this new development will damage my prospects with Lucy even further unless I succeed. As I approached my front gate I saw the ancient Mrs. Zell, my landlady, on the front walk. With some obvious revulsion, she was examining something on the ground near the porch stairs. She looked up and saw me and waved urgently for me to hurry to her.

"I'll swan I've never *seen* such an ugly thing!" she said. She seemed awestruck and unwilling to take her eyes off the thing on the ground.

"What is it?" I could just see part of it behind a boxwood bush.

"I never *seen* such a thing. It's some ugly little thing, some little *dead* thing." Mrs. Zell's manner of speaking is to emphasize at least one word in every phrase or sentence. "What *is* that? I wonder how long it's *been* there? I *never* noticed it until just now."

"It looks like it's been dead a while," I said. "Maybe the cat dragged it here?" That prospect seemed unlikely. The creature was not as large as a cat but looked formidable. It was unlike anything I had ever seen. It was hairless except for a few patches of a gray, coarse fur near its hindquarters and on its feet… its *six* feet. It had forepaws armed with long, curved talons and two sets of hind legs, similarly armed. There was a short set of hind legs in front of a longer, more powerful set. The short legs seemed to be vestigial or perhaps some sort of malformation, because like the forelimbs of the great Tyrannosaurs found in the West lately, they seemed to have no practical use.

The head of the creature was beyond classification. It had a short, muzzle-less face, two bulging eyes, filmy and gray in death, and a round mouth much like a lamprey's with many needle-like teeth. Below the weak jaw were two appendages tipped with bony barbs, that reminded me of the stinger of a scorpion. Its skin was gray with a bluish tinge, sagging and wrinkled and showing the first stages of decay.

"It's a chimera," I said. "I've never seen such a collection of deformities. What *is* it? We had many monstrous specimens in jars at the university, but nothing like this. Doesn't have much of a smell, does it?"

"I can't *touch* it," Mrs. Zell moaned. "Please get *rid* of it for me, Mr. Jarre."

"I wonder if we should notify someone? Some county official or the sheriff, or even one of my old professors at the Carthesian University?"

"I don't want to *see* it again. Just dispose of it *immediately*, please, and . . . why are you home from work in the *middle* of the morning?"

You may remember my interest in natural history and zoology. It was I who always cared for the war horses when I had the chance and looked after cats and dogs displaced by battle. In school, I loved zoology more than chemistry, my major field of study, but couldn't foresee a way to make a living at it. I could not see myself dumping this horrific and unique creature in a grave, or disposing of it in the city dump. I assured Mrs. Zell I would dispose of the dead thing.

I went up to my room and found an old lidded laboratory jar with a two-gallon volume I had retrieved from the lab after Karl threw it out. I had a supply of denatured alcohol, too, which I had brought home for cleaning and as lamp fuel. I poured about a gallon of this into the jar. In the shed back near the alley, I found a burlap sack and a shovel. From just outside the kitchen window I could hear Mrs. Zell speaking to her niece on the telephone, telling her the story of the discovery.

I slid the shovel under the body of the creature and lifted gently. It was so fragile with putrefaction that the gray skin tore as I lifted, revealing a swarming and disgusting mass of maggots inside. My gorge rose and I thought I might eject my breakfast on the spot! It seemed odd to me that with the weather turning colder the maggots would still be active in the body, but I soon saw a wisp of steam rise from the torn skin as though the body were still warm inside. As I held the top of the sack open and passed the laden shovel under it, one of the barbs on the creature's jaw scraped below my left thumb. I gently lay the burden inside the sack and immediately started to notice that the punctured place on my hand was going numb. By the time I lifted the sack off the ground, my left hand had gone completely dead and had become nearly useless. I reckoned the barbs deliver some sort of anesthetic or paralytic agent, as some insects and spiders do, which may aid in the killing of its prey.

I carried my burden up the front stairs so Mrs. Zell would not see me. Once in my room I locked my door and lowered the sack into the jar which I had placed on my work table. With a set of shears, I split the sack on both sides of the carcass and with a little twitching of the sack, the body slipped out. It drifted gracefully into the fluid, tatters of decayed flesh fluttering about it like tiny wings. One of the small rear legs fell off and wafted slowly to the bottom of the jar. The body settled against the side of the glass: its head and left shoulder near the top of the surface of the alcohol, and its hindquarters resting on the bottom. Soon the body and the fluid into which it had been placed, were still. Its filmy eyes seemed to be looking at me. By this time, I had begun to notice the feeling returning to my left thumb.

I turned my desk chair around and sat in it, looking at the jar. The eyes of the creature still seemed fixed on me; they were an opaque gray-blue. I was struck again at what a chimera the thing is, at what impossible biological inheritances had come together so unbelievably and implausibly to create it. Now, at least, it is preserved in its jar and it will decompose no more but remain forever in its present suspended state until I can decipher its mysteries further. I think you will be the only person I tell about this thing, George, at least for now. I will cover the jar with a sheet when I am away. I cover the whole table most of the time, and the Morstan girl who cleans up for Mrs. Zell never disturbs the sheet when she's in here. I think there is little chance she will discover my secret.

Yours,
Abel

November 22, 1922

George:
I wonder when you will receive my last letter and what your response will be? I hope you will respond, as I would like to have your reaction and opinion of the little dead thing. I will try to sketch it today and include that with this message.

The first action of a man displaced from his livelihood is to try to find his next employment in that same field. There is a limeworks in Ste. Odile, Seraphim Lime, it's called. Their offices and small laboratory are on Mal Ardents Street. I walked there after mailing Friday's letter. Mr. Arnot, who is in charge of the office and laboratory, agreed to see me, if grudgingly. His office is a glass-walled cubicle and it was freezing in there. He asked me to sit in an oaken chair opposite his desk. His face was purple and his corduroy vest could scarcely contain his stomach.

"Abel Jarre," he said. "I have heard of you."

"I am surprised."

"Yes, I am in the Knights of Columbus, and one of my brothers there is Mr. Karl, your former supervisor."

"Ah." I felt my prospects here fade suddenly away. "I am surprised my name should come up between Lodge brothers."

"He mentioned you Friday night, the day he dismissed you. He thought you might come here seeking work."

I felt the anger rise inside me but I did my best to suppress it. "So, he was warning you then," I said.

"He said you were not gregarious, not a joiner or a mixer. In fact, he said you have an argumentative and disagreeable nature. He mentioned you as a free thinker, an eccentric..."

"He and I have had our disagreements. I am nervous, high strung as my Lieutenant Allen used to say. But... I am not an atheist, if that's what you mean by 'free thinker,' sir. Far from it."

"I don't see you in church. You're not a Protestant, are you? In which case, you are as *good* as an atheist."

"No, I was raised a Catholic. I speak to God in my own way. A more personal way. In the war, I started to see God differently than I had before, and I saw... that He wishes me to understand Him in a new light, different from the manner in which I was raised."

"That does sound a little eccentric to me," Arnot stifled a yawn. "We all need the Church whether we know it or not. Those who think otherwise are mistaken. Pure and simple. Isn't up to each of us to interpret Scripture. Then everyone would do whatever they wanted. You are a single man... yes?"

"Yes. I have asked a young lady to marry me but she hasn't answered me yet. If I get a new position, perhaps..."

"Karl told me you were in the 111th Pennsylvania. How did that come about?"

"There was nothing for me here... at the time. I had no family, or... I went to Pittsburgh for a new start, to see if I could work in the laboratory of a coal company, but the only job I could get was as a hand loader under-ground. Backbreaking work. Then we got into the war."

Arnot looked at me as though he either didn't believe my story or was not the least interested in it, I couldn't tell which.

"I know you have experience and I could make a place for you immediately," he finally said, "but I have to think about it. It's a small space here to be closed up together all day. I don't like to rock the boat. A different personality can rock the boat. I didn't want to take Karl's word alone about you. I wanted to hear your responses to his assertions for myself. I am a fair man, and as I said, there is work you could do now. But . . . I don't know. Let me think it over. Your boarding house has a telephone? I will call in a few days if I decide to proceed. Thank you for coming in, Mr. Jarre."

It had turned much colder in the brief time I had been at Seraphim. The walk home took me past Boyer's Butcher Shop and I thought of stopping in to ask if there was any work available there, but I argued with Boyer a year ago about some spoiled mutton he sold me, and he has never seemed to like me much since. And besides, I was anxious to get back to my room to study the creature more and sketch it for you.

Before I could get back home, it began to snow; large, fluffy flakes that quickly blanketed grass, trees, and the brick, stone, and iron fences and gates of Ste. Odile. I stood on the front porch of the boarding house watching the snow fall. I was transfixed by the look of it, by the beautiful silence, and only when it struck me how cold my face and feet were did I realize I must have been standing there for a very long time. I find that my attention wanders more and more lately, and I often forget what I am about. Back in my room I uncovered the jar and for all the world I could swear that the creature had moved a little. Its head seemed deeper below the surface of the alcohol and its left forelimb wasn't in the same position as before.

Its eyes had seemed to move too. I stared at it in mild disbelief for fully five minutes, but I detected no twitch or tremor. The animal's filmy orbs seemed to be looking deeply into my own eyes. As I stood looking down at it on the tabletop, it was peering directly back at me. When I pulled my chair next to the table, sat and looked at it again, it was still looking at me. I sat as still as I could for thirty minutes and didn't take my eyes off of it. I saw not the slightest suggestion of movement. I removed my sketching diary from my desk, found a pencil and started to draw the thing. As I sketched, concentrating on getting just the right curvature of the odd skull, in my peripheral vision, I thought I perceived the creature twitch slightly. When I looked directly at it I could see there was some little disturbance to the liquid in the jar, but saw no sign of change in the creature.

The snow continued to fall heavily. There are but a handful of automobiles in Ste. Odile, and I could hear that one of them had become stuck in a snow bank on the street below. I looked out my window and saw the yellow Packard of Robert Dufresne half-buried in a drift, tires spinning uselessly. This was the same Dufresne I mentioned in a letter of last spring who objected to my membership in the Ste. Odile Ethical Union and was solely responsible for my rejected application. He got out of his car and examined his predicament. The solution, of course, was a push. He was in need of someone to push him out. After a second he glanced upward and saw me looking at him from my window. After a few seconds more, when I was sure he recognized me, I turned and resumed my seat. Did I do the wrong thing, George? It was spitefulness, wasn't it? It was a prideful and vengeful sin and I wish now I had done otherwise.

I heard a rustle of paper behind me. I turned to see that Mrs. Zell or one of her girls had slipped a note under my door. It was from Lucy. It read:

Dear Abel:
My family has helped me realize that the affection I have felt for you for the past year is more in the nature of friendship than romantic love. I am honored by your proposal of marriage, but given the limitations of my feelings for you, I know it would be a mistake to accept it, one which we would both soon regret. In addition, we have heard of your being terminated from your job, news which further sullies any notion of a comfortable future with you which any woman might entertain. My greatest wish is that you find a lady who can return your feelings in kind. Thank you for your attentions to me and best of luck.
Your Friend,
Lucy

So, there was my answer. I am a poor prospect, and it seems she never loved me anyway! I always suspected as much, and her note came as no great surprise. Still, it was painful, to see it written out like that. I will go for a walk in a little while and try to clear my head or distract my thoughts, whichever seems more appropriate at the time. I sat back down at my desk.

I added a few finishing touches to my sketch of the creature. Satisfied I had reproduced it accurately, I will include it with this letter and get it in the mail to you.

Sincerely, Abel

December 4, 1922

George:

It has been so long since I have heard from you. I check the mail anxiously every day, and with some excitement, yet nothing comes. Of course, Mrs. Zell knows of my unemployment now. She has said if I have no new job by the end of this month, she would prefer that I find other lodgings because she has no place for transients— as I will shortly be! No house will take in an unemployed man when I am put out of here, so it is becoming almost certain that I must leave town.

Yet, I start every day with more hope than the day proves to warrant. There is expectation of some boon or positive helpful thing, that *could* happen, but what that could specifically be, I cannot define. All I know is that no such thing *does* happen. Every day is the same. I awake at four or five in the morning. I toast some bread and fry an egg for my breakfast and I sit for an hour or more and look at the dead thing in the jar. I still have no notion of what it is or where it fits into Nature. I sketched it again and sent that to John Stubbs, one of my zoology professors at Carthesian, but no response yet. He may think I am trying out some practical joke on him. I will need to buy a camera and photograph it.

The most striking thing about the creature, I say again, is what an impossible mixture of heritages it is. It defies what little I understand about genetical science. I wonder how intelligent it was. I wonder if it had thought processes of a predator, which are necessarily more complex than those of prey animals. And I wondered where more of the species might be or if it was the last of its kind. I still own a copy of *The Classification of Higher Vertebrates* by Hawkins, from my undergraduate days, and an antique copy of *Compendium Naturalis Mundi* by Van der Meet which I found in a bookseller's stall a few years ago in St. Louis. I found nothing in either of these which in any way corresponds to my creature. I walked to the small Ste. Odile public library on Bucephalus Street, but their sad collection of volumes on natural history also contained no reference or image of anything I could relate to my animal. I hope that Stubbs will take an interest and help me with this. Perhaps my letter will induce him to come look at it, as I can't quite imagine carrying the jar with me on the train. On my way home from the library, I asked for work at the bakery and Broussard's Pharmacy, but was given no encouragement from either. Back at home I clipped tatters of flesh from the creature in three different places and have prepared slides for such a time when I may have access to a microscope and examine them in detail, or send them to Stubbs for examination.

I watch the thing and watch it. Sometimes for a moment I am distracted by something, perhaps something I have never noticed before in my surroundings. Something unextraordinary elsewhere in my room like the smoothness of my desktop or the weight of my pocket watch or penknife, or even re-reading Lucy's note, and my attention wanders. It is only at those times that I think I notice that the thing moves, almost imperceptibly. If there is some spark of life in it and it wishes to deceive me, it is failing at that, because I know what I am seeing is real.

And at night in my bed when the room is dark, I sometimes think I hear the movement of liquid, a slight sloshing sound, but I can't be sure about that. At those moments, it seems there is no other sound in the world, no human activity in the street, no animal noise or boats on the river, nothing but the sound in the jar, that *liquid* sound. A terror strikes me that if the thing would turn out to be alive, the lid of the jar could not contain it, and in the dark while I sleep, it could be abroad in the room with me. By the time I get the light on to investigate, there is nothing to be seen. Then I must take some of my bromide to settle into sleep again.

Dec. 5

I have started to duplicate everything I have written you in a journal. I wanted to have my own copy of this experience, otherwise it may be lost. It seems less likely every week that you will ever answer these letters.

I should start packing my things, but most days I don't have the energy or concentration to do it. Mrs. Zell hardly speaks to me at all now, except to remind me of what day of the month it is. I told her I have inquired at most of the other boarding houses in town but they either have no room for me or do not want me. I continue to have no luck in finding any kind of job. Since my dismissal from Osage Lead, my reputation has spread across town. An undeserved reputation, an unfair one, I hope. I should consider moving to St. Louis or maybe back to Pittsburgh. The society of this little town is closed and unwelcoming. Humans are social creatures and when an individual is ostracized by his group and cast out, it leaves an emptiness in his soul which defies description. There is no more certain way to kill a man that that, I think. I have a little more than thirty dollars to my name.

Yes, I should begin packing but sometimes I don't think I move for hours at a stretch. From time to time I wonder if I should go out or stay in. I ask myself where I would go if I went out? If I went out I would pass men in the streets who have wives and families, friends and coworkers. Yes, they have all of those gifts from above, they have a place in the order of things, the clear and well-understood blessing of God. I will not have my Lucy, nor anyone else, most likely. So, it seems to me now. But none of those men have what I have. None of them have this secret. I stare for hours at the thing in the jar because now I know, I am sure, it must be watching me. I want to *see* it move directly, not *suspect* it has moved. I want to know unambiguously that there is some little glimmer of life in it. I possess this thing. I have a connection to it and no one else on earth may say that. If my prospects are few and unpromising, maybe there is some way I can exploit that connection, or use it to secure some livelihood, some sort of future for myself? This creature was put in front of me for a reason, surely. Finding it, classifying it and describing it to the world is obviously what I am meant to do. Most of the time I am certain of this. Other times I am not so sure. Maybe exploitation of this animal would be wrong. I am a private man. Maybe God put it in my way *because* I am so private. Maybe God's plan for me in His creation has always been with regard to this creature. It is so hard to know what God wants. Why would this responsibility be given to me? The only reason I can imagine is that this is the answer I have been seeking these four years. I just have to *understand* it.

I will go to sleep now. The silence is what is so oppressive. Any little sound can become frightening, can seem to be a threat or be distorted by my imagination. Did I hear the lid of the jar move? Did I hear the movement of liquid? If I hear activity on the street or the sounds of other people in the house, any troubling sound is masked or hidden. There is none of that now, so I try to sleep so I will hear nothing that will unsettle me. Tomorrow I will pawn anything I still have which may be of value and pack my things. I will buy a train ticket to St. Louis. It appears I must go to St. Louis.

Later:

This morning I carried a bundle of things with me to LaHaye's Pawn Shop on Rouen Street close by. I took some trouble to bring some lidded jars and an old burner and even my copy of Van der Meet, which I thought might be of some value. LaHaye scowled and studied the things and in the end refused to buy anything I had brought. Now what am I to do? I will soon have no place to live and no means of establishing myself elsewhere.

Afternoon:

George, the creature moved! Just as I was awakening from a nap, I saw it, clearly and without doubt. It twitched and some white particles floated up from the tear in its skin. A stab of terror shot through my stomach as I watched it floating in its liquid until the ripples in the jar subsided. Slowly I got out of my bed and approached it. Now its filmy eye did not seem to be watching me, but only staring vacantly at the wall behind me. As I neared the jar I could see that the white particles which had floated up from the tear in the creature's skin were bitten-off fragments of the maggots I had seen inside it the day I recovered it from under the bush. Slowly and carefully, I lifted the heavy lid from the jar and looked down at the thing inside. I looked into the torn flesh of the back. The tissue inside it was a nondescript blue-gray confusion of subcutaneous fat and muscle and collapsing gray blood vessels. But something else beyond these caught my attention. It was a familiar shape, but one I could not quite define or make sense of. Suddenly the shape quivered and slid downward across a glistening and awakening orb. It was an eyelid blinking across a yellow, sensate eye!

I withdrew in horror and disgust across the room from the thing. I stood at my window looking back at it trying to understand what I had seen. I was breathing frantically. I tried to steady myself. After a few moments, I approached the table again, slowly and tentatively. I looked down into the jar. The tear in the dead creature's skin was a little wider and cleaner now, and I could see that this was so because the smaller one inside had eaten away the edges of the wound. Shivering with revulsion I looked at it and in a moment its minute wriggling and writhing to feed revealed that it was an immature version of the dead thing which had served as its host. I clapped the lid back on the jar and withdrew again to my window. I sat at my desk, never taking my eyes off the jar.

This was the creature's nature. It reproduced itself by growing an embryo inside which slowly consumed the host body of the mother: a type of matriphagy as some spiders practice. Or perhaps this carcass was the father and the fertilized zygote is placed within him while he is alive, to grow as is seen in some marine animals, I believe. The males in nature are usually more disposable than females. This conjecture makes the most sense to me. And the growing fetus must be anaerobic if circumstances warrant even after it is viable, otherwise it could never survive in the alcohol.

A knock at my door. "Mr. Jarre?" It was Mrs. Zell. "I have a *letter* here for you. Just arrived." She pushed it under the door. "And Mr. *Jarre,* I have a young lady coming up from Cape Girardeau on Monday. Miss *Connolly* is her name. She is to be the new *housekeeper* at the rectory. I want her to have *this* room. I would be *obliged* if you could be out by the weekend."

"But I was counting on having the full month, Mrs. Zell."

"We rent by the *week*, Mr. Jarre. I can put you out at my *discretion.* By the weekend, if you *please.*"

"I need more time, Mrs. Zell. I have nowhere to go."

"To be *honest*, Mr. Jarre, I regretted bringing you in here almost *immediately.* You have always been an *ill* fit. I don't know *why* you would want to stay in a *house* or a *town* for that matter, where you weren't wanted. I shouldn't repeat this, but now I hear from Mrs. *LaHaye* that you have tried to sell goods to her *husband* which were obviously stolen from your last employer. She believes Mr. Karl has pressed a complaint against you, and the Sheriff has a *warrant* for your arrest which he will execute when he returns from that *shooting* business on DeCastres Island in a day or two. Perhaps I shouldn't have *mentioned* it but I have always spoken *plainly,* and you are hardly in a position to run away from the *justice* awaiting you . . . and I suppose you have a right to know. I will have no *undesirables* in my house."

I am to be arrested? The old woman's words were like a judgment from heaven. It was like that moment on the transport ship when we realized that the war made us understand everything in a new way. The entire town wants me gone, and I have no means to go elsewhere. So, what will I do?

There was a slight sloshing sound in the jar. I could see the gray, slippery body of the dead thing twitch a little as the offspring inside it fed. I arose and went to my door, picking up the letter Mrs. Zell had pushed under it. It was from Professor Stubbs at Carthesian. It said:

Mr. Jarre:
You claim to have been in a vertebrate zoology class of mine some ten years ago, but I have no memory of you. Your letter is obviously a hoax as the creature you describe is a biological impossibility, as someone with a true knowledge of natural history would certainly

know. Please find better ways to occupy your time than by dreaming up nonsense to waste the time of persons more productive than your-self.

    Signed,

    J.S.

So, there it is, George. I am soon to be homeless or arrested, and I have no prospects but to take this thing in its jar and try to show some scientific or academic person that it is real and I have made a great discovery. But who will listen? I am exhausted. I must rest.

Dec. 7

George: This will be my last letter. I will leave it on my table for Mrs. Zell to find. And what *else* will she find? I am not well. I am not strong, but I am content. I feel such peace now. I am holding a towel to my face as I write. My face is numb but bloody. Covered in blood. I slept a deep undrugged sleep last night. I scarcely moved all night and only awoke ten minutes ago. As I started to awaken, I noticed that the lower half of my face was numb, completely without feeling. There was a small weight on my chest and neck. As my eyes slowly focused, I was horrified to see the young creature from the jar sitting on my chest, just at the collarbone. Its dark eyes watched me indifferently. Its small body was a perfect copy of its dead parent except it had more fur. Its mouth and face were covered in blood. My blood! It had deadened my face with its stingers! I gasped and choked on the blood I inhaled with the breath. I jumped out of my bed and saw that the mattress was splattered in red. The little thing fell to the floor with a soft, flopping thud, and seemed unhurt and unperturbed.

I pressed myself to the wall and moved away from it to my front door. I opened the door and looking out

---

89

into the hallway, I could see no one was about. Mrs. Zell was probably downstairs and it was too early for the Morstan girl to come and clean. I slipped down the hallway to the lavatory and turned on the light. To my horror I saw that my lips had been eaten away in a ragged pattern revealing bloody teeth within. A little cry escaped my tattered mouth, spattering blood on the mirror.

At first, I could not think of what to do. I could not think of calling Mrs. Zell, or returning to my room. After a few minutes, I made my way back down the hallway to my door. My fear and sense of revulsion had suddenly subsided. Now I could not define how I was feeling, except to say there was no panic. I was suddenly calm and clear-headed. I opened my door and edged into my room. The little creature was still where it had fallen, and seemed completely oblivious to me.

I watched it for many minutes. It was cleaning the blood from the edges of its mouth. It seemed so purposeful and focused on its natural function, on the undoubted, perfect fulfillment of its nature: its God-ordained purpose, as the Bible says. I don't know if I smiled at it or not as I peacefully watched it. If I did, it would not have been recognizable as a smile. I locked my door and braced my one dining chair against the knob. I sat at my desk and wrote this account for you. This action, this perfect, natural action had begun and I must not interfere with it. I am filled with the love of God at this moment, and so grateful for His blessing . . . George, my friend . . . or one whom I once thought of that way, a deep, deep sleep is what is needed, that I may better comply with my part in this. My bromide powder is on the table . . .

John S. McFarland's first novel, *The Black Garden* was published in 2010 to universal praise. His work has appeared in *The Twilight Zone Magazine*, *Eldritch Tales*, *National Lampoon*, *River Styx*, *Tornado Alley*, and in six anthologies, including *A Treasury of American Horror Stories*, along with work by Stephen King and H. P. Lovecraft. He has written extensively on historical and arts-related subjects and has been a guest lecturer in fiction at Washington University in St. Louis. He is a lifelong Bigfoot enthusiast, and *Annette: A Big, Hairy Mom* is his first novel for young readers. Its sequel will appear in 2017.

VESSEL

by Ibai Canales

The first thing he thought was, "I must be dead. I must be having one of those out-of-body experiences people with near-death experiences talk about."

There was no other way to explain why he was staring down at his own face. How did it happen? He tried to remember, but it was all blurry. He had wanted to stay in the temple while all the others retreated to the camp to celebrate the finding, he remembered that much. He wanted to study the machinery and the . . .

The bodies.

What if they were still alive, as Alice had suggested? What if one of them had somehow woken up and attacked him? He had been, after all, trying to discern if the machines that encased them worked. He remembered having ran his gloved fingers carefully over the intricate hieroglyphs on what seemed to be the control panel when . . . When what? He could remember no more.

He heard voices coming down from the shaft and felt a sudden burst of hope. He didn't know what he hoped for, he doubted anyone on the team had the ability to re-insert his soul into his dead body, as impressive as everyone's credentials were, but at least he wouldn't have to face death alone.

"Augie?" he heard Ryerson call. He hated it. His name was Augustus, and he was proud of it. "Augie, are you all right?"

He tried to speak, but no sound came out of his mouth. Of course, now that he was a ghost, he would probably need a Ouija board to communicate with the living.

The first one to come down the shaft and into the chamber was Ryerson himself, closely followed by Alice and Bellowo, the South African geologist.

Ryerson, despite being the fine specimen of an American male that he was, square jaw and closely cropped blond hair included, looked smaller than usual. The horrified look in his face also made him look younger.

"We picked up an energy surge coming from the chamber, did you? . . ." Alice suddenly stopped talking and mimicked Ryerson's petrified expression.

"My God," the South African geologist whispered.

They could see him? Maybe he was an apparition, floating over his own dead body. He was ready to consider that possibility, he had become surprisingly open minded in the last few minutes.

"They're still alive," Alice said, instinctively seeking refuge behind Ryerson's powerful shoulder.

"No sudden moves," Ryerson said quietly.

What the hell were they talking about? He tried to ask them, but again, he found himself unable to produce a sound.

"My god," the geologist repeated. "He's dead. They killed him."

"Stay calm," Ryerson whispered, extending his arms as if they were a barrier to keep the two scientists away from him.

"Calm?" Alice let out a nervous giggle. "They're alive and they're hostile . . ."

"Shut up," Ryerson grunted impatiently, "Don't startle him. Bellowo, go get the shotgun. Slowly."

Agustus watched Bellowo walk slowly up the shaft, and nearly tripping and falling because the geologist was unable to take his bloodshot eyes away from him while he did so.

He wanted to ask them what they were so damn afraid of. It was him, good old Augustus Cripps, albeit in spectral form. He couldn't look so bad, could he? Surely not something out of those horror movies his nephew liked so much . . .

He raised his hands to look at them. He was half-expecting a couple of glowing, skeletal extremities, but instead, he found himself looking at what could only be described as black fins. Two black, shiny, shapeless lumps.

Like the ones the corpses in the chambers had.

"Oh God," he thought. "Oh God, this can't be happening . . ."

But it was. He looked down at his new body. It wasn't translucent or glowing at all. It was black and chitinous. He raised his so-called hands to touch his face, but he already knew what he was going to find: the smooth, featureless surface he had seen on the other creatures.

"Oh Christ, I'm one of them."

How did this happen? He staggered toward Ryerson and Alice, raising his tentacle-like arms toward them. "Help me," he tried to say, but the black plate he had for a face wouldn't allow any sounds. Come to think of that, he wasn't sure this new body he was in had any vocal cords. As he approached the pair, he realized he was now much taller. He looked down on them as they walked away from him, Alice frantically holding Ryerson's arm.

"Oh God, it's coming after us!"

"Bellowo!" Ryerson yelled, not taking his eyes away from Augustus' now featureless face.

"Here!" the geologist replied, and Augustus could see the Mossberg 500 shotgun fly down the shaft. Ryerson skillfully grabbed it in midair, cocked it and shot Augustus right where his stomach would have been. The shot made the ancient walls of the chamber tremble like a tuning fork.

It didn't hurt. It felt like a punch in the gut, but it didn't hurt. Panic took hold of Augustus' mind as he found himself flying across the room with a gaping, smoking hole right in the middle of his torso.

"Oh my God, now I'm really going to die," he thought. "I'm really going to die."

But he didn't. He crashed against one of the glass niches that harbored the alien bodies and fell on the dusty floor only to immediately jump back up and run towards the lower levels of the temple. He didn't know what he would find. He didn't know what he was doing. He didn't know anything at all, except that he wanted to get as far as possible from Ryerson and his shotgun.

Ryerson fired again. The shot made a good chunk of primeval rock fall over his black, armored head, which only stoked the flames of his terror. With the sound of the shotgun and Alice's voice begging Ryerson to leave still ringing in his now non-existent ears, Augustus got lost in the darkness.

He came back to his senses as a man who suddenly wakes up from a nightmare. He realized two things: one, he didn't know how long he had been there, cowering in the darkness of the lower levels. Two, he was stuck to the stone ceiling like some kind of massive alien spider.

He looked at the amorphous extremities that were his arms. They had sprouted long, curved claws that had sunken themselves in the stone.

The shock of seeing that made his limbs go flaccid. He fell from the ceiling and onto the floor. Yet again, he felt no pain.

"Is this normal?" he thought. "Am I supposed to be insensitive to pain now, or am I just in shock?"

That reminded him of the gaping wound on his torso. Feeling the grip of terror again, he looked down at it. It was already closing. The healing process was so fast, he could actually witness as it happened, like a blood stain spreading in reverse. What had he become? And how did it happen? Suddenly, he felt a suffocating rush of claustrophobia, except it wasn't the ancient, hieroglyph-laden corridor that was oppressing him. It was his own body. The black, chitinous obscenity he had suddenly found himself trapped in. Along with the claustrophobia, he felt a wave of repulsion. He clawed at his armored head, at his bulbous thorax. The wounds closed instantly as if they were liquid. He tried to scream, but couldn't produce a sound.

Out. Out. Out. He had to get out of that thing.

"Calm down, old man," he told himself, when the terror subsided, even though he couldn't vocalize the words. "Think. Go back to the beginning."

He had wanted to stay in the temple a bit longer to study the hieroglyphs. They had spent six weeks in the desert, fruitlessly digging for any traces of the fabled god-like entities the natives talked about, and they had finally hit the motherlode. No, just five hours in that chamber wasn't enough for him. He was on the verge of cracking the language. He was close to understanding what creatures—that had walked the planet eons before the first humans climbed down the trees—had to say. He was the best in his field, and he was about to prove it. Augustus Cripps, dead language expert, was about to decipher a language that was more than dead: everyone who spoke it had been grinded to dust ages before the first human being walked the Earth.

Everyone except the dark, faceless creatures in the glass niches, of course.

He now remembered he had made a substantial mistake: he wasn't dealing with primitive humans. He was dealing with a species that was far more advanced than humans currently were. He wasn't reading a story, the rise and fall of some mighty pre-human king, or the legend of their sun-god. This read more like . . . a user's manual. He had a clear memory of his finger unwittingly pressing a rhomboidal knob on the dark metallic panel and then . . .

He had woken up inside of one of the alien bodies encased in the glass niches. He had been unknowingly operating an alien machine. And it had somehow transferred his consciousness into this thing. Under other circumstances, he would have felt marveled at the thought of a species that had been able to unravel the mysteries of consciousness, to the point of being able to transfer it to... What was it that he was now anyway? Some type of living tool? A battle suit, perhaps? Not only was he now impervious to pain and had amazingly quick healing capabilities, he also noticed that he hadn't taken a single breath of air since he had woken up inside his new body (not that he would be able to, without the necessary orifices), so there was a fair chance that he was inside the alien equivalent of an extreme environment suit.

But suits could be taken off, couldn't they? If the machine had transferred his mind into this slimy, featureless monstrosity, maybe it could transfer it back to his old body.

He needed to go back to the upper chamber, he needed to finish deciphering the instructions in the panel.

And of course, he would need to retrieve his body.

As he had expected, they had taken it with them, and of course, they had blocked the shaft that led down to the temple. Ryerson might have been a simple man, but he was no fool, and always prepared for the worst. They had driven one of the 4x4 Fords to the entrance and then they had flipped it over so the roof would cover it. Those 6000 pounds of metal posed an insurmountable challenge for anyone who tried to move them. Unfortunately for Ryerson and the others, he wasn't planning on moving them. He was planning on going through them.

He looked at one of his ever-fluctuating limbs and ordered it to change. Practice paid off, and it quickly became a long, obsidian-colored blade. He knew from experience that his claws could penetrate the stone and the alien metal of the inner chambers of the temple, so there was no reason why he couldn't do the same to the roof of the Ford.

He was right. His scythe easily went through the aluminum surface and lodged itself into the top of the driver's seat. He retracted it a few inches, and then quickly drew a circle on the roof. He peeled the metal circle with surprising ease (he was much stronger now, as he had anticipated) and entered the vehicle. He smashed the windshield with one of his boneless elbows (which had become suddenly hard for the occasion) and stepped out of the mound in which they had found the ancient structure and into the desert.

Of course, there would be guards.

The two bearded men instantly began yelling and pointing their antique rifles at him. Augustus immediately recognized them as two of the native carriers they had hired at a nearby village.

He had been studying the local dialect during their flight from Paris, and despite the fact that he was still struggling with the pronunciation, he clearly understood that they were afraid of the sand demon that stole the souls of men.

Had this happened before? Maybe some villager had discovered the temple by chance, accessed the corpse chamber and gone through the same body-swapping process he'd gone through? He wanted to ask them, but again, the smooth, featureless plate he had for a face prevented him from uttering a sound. He instead raised his formless limbs in a surrendering gesture, but apparently, that only made him look more menacing. The two men become frantic, their speech garbled and unintelligible, and before he could do anything else to calm them down, one of them had already fired his rifle. He felt the impact on his face plate and for a second, the world became fuzzy and sort of pixelated.

"I'm artificial," he thought distractedly. "I'm some kind of organic robot."

Then he heard the dribbling sound, looked to his left, and realized that the bullet had somehow bounced off his head and hit the Ford's gas tank. A puddle of fuel was forming in the sand right next to him.

The men were still frantic. The one who had shot him cocked his rifle, ready to fire another round.

Augustus raised his tentacles once again, trying to warn him. His panic turned them into a pair of grotesque, black trees.

Both guards screamed in terror at the sight. They began shooting wildly.

The Ford exploded.

He was on fire. The thought repeated over and over in his mind like an insane mantra. *I'm on fire. I'm on fire. I'm on fire.*

Engulfed in flames, Augustus ran mindlessly through the camp. He finally hit a tent and fell on the sand. He became embroiled in nylon, cord, and the smell of his own charred flesh (yes, somehow his new body allowed him the sense of smell, and it smelt surprisingly similar to fried calamari). The tent covering him combined with his frantic thrashing finally stifled the flames, which allowed him to recover a semblance of self-control.

Giving thanks to whichever deity took care of alien artificial creatures for the absolute lack of pain, he stood up. Trying to ascertain the damage done, he looked down at his body. His flesh, which until a minute ago had been black and slimy, was now greyish and brittle.

He heard a human voice roar. Before he could ascertain its origin, he saw a mattock descend and lodge itself into his chest. He became paralyzed with horror. His mind flooded with a silent scream. He was being stabbed. For some reason, the thought was worse than the one of being shot at or set ablaze. It was almost offensive.

He was being stabbed, for God's sake!

"Die, you bastard!" Ryerson screamed, as he drove the mattock into his chest, his left shoulder, his back as he instinctively turned away from the attack.

He fell on his belly and tried to crawl away from the onslaught, but he could still feel the point of the mattock go in and out of his back.

"Kill it!" He heard Alice say. "Remember what it did to Augie!"

He was in the middle of pondering how long it would be before Ryerson found a vulnerable spot in his new anatomy when he heard Alice say his name. Something clicked inside his head, and he felt a sudden surge of rage amidst the cloud of terror that crippled his mind.

My name is Augustus, you dumb bitch, he thought, as he ordered his left arm to become a scythe. He rolled over and drove it into Ryerson's chest as he was lifting the mattock for a new blow.

The chief archaeologist fell limply beside him, raising a small cloud of sand.

Alice began screaming. She screamed, and screamed, and screamed.

For a second, Augustus had begun to feel a euphoric feeling of triumph: he had bested someone in combat, something that he, a bookish, sickly man, had only been able to dream of. Then, the sound of Alice's screams made his pride go cold and turn to horror once again. What had he done? He had murdered a man. He had taken a life. He was no longer innocent. No longer a good man.

He had to do something about it. He had to make things right again. But how? He needed to think. But she wouldn't shut up . . .

Without putting much thought into what he was doing, he raised one of his limbs toward Alice. It elongated and flew towards her, and it covered her mouth neatly, creating a perfect cast of her lower jaw.

That didn't calm her one bit. Quite the contrary, actually, as she began convulsing and clawing at his grotesquely long forearm.

Augustus raised his other tentacle and produced a morbid finger, which then proceeded to fall right in front of where his mouth was supposed to be, hoping to mimic the silence gesture.

Alice rolled her eyes into her head and fainted.

Augustus panicked again. Was she dead? Had he killed her?

He retracted his tentacle and walked fearfully toward her. Dear God, maybe he had suffocated her. He didn't know what his body could or couldn't do. Maybe he had invaded her throat and choked her.

He produced yet another finger and put it under her ear. No, her heart was still beating. She had just passed out due to the shock.

He hated not being able to let out a sigh of relief.

"Get away from her!"

He turned around to face Bellowo. The guards had obviously run away, but they had left their rifles behind. Bellowo was holding one of them.

"I won't let you hurt her." He tried to sound stern, but his fear was palpable. Like himself, Bellowo was a scholar, not a man of action. He had probably never fired a gun before in his life, as his shaking hands showed. The barrel of the rifle danced almost comically.

Augustus slowly walked away from Alice and raised his arms. Could Bellowo be the key to solving everything? He had only known him since the expedition began, but they had gotten along almost immediately. They were both middle-aged, single, and more passionate about their jobs than about their respective social lives. Neither of them really liked Ryerson.

"What are you doing?" Bellowo asked nervously. "Are you . . . Are you surrendering?"

Augustus had an idea. He kneeled and had his right tentacle produce a sharp tip. He dug it into the sand, and immediately heard Bellowo hold his breath. He could almost feel the geologist's thoughts. Was this some kind of cunning alien strategy?

Augustus began drawing a big, capital I. Then an A.

"Wait . . ." Bellowo lowered the rifle. "Are you trying to communicate?"

Yes! There was hope after all. Bellowo would listen. After all, Bellowo was like him.

He was about to finish drawing the big M when he heard shots being fired once again. He raised his head and saw a bunch of natives running toward them. They were carrying torches and more ancient firearms, no doubt leftovers from the last war.

It seemed that the guards had not ran away after all. They had simply gone to get reinforcements. He could hear their angry voices, caught loose words, and they didn't sound particularly imaginative. They were, basically, out to hunt and kill the soul-stealing demon.

Something whistled through the night air. Augustus felt the blow on his left shoulder and shortly after, he heard the shot. Then he heard the natives cheering. Alice stirred, opened her eyes and resumed her screaming the second she set them on him.

Bellowo looked at her, then he looked at Augustus with a puzzled expression. He raised his rifle once again.

"Don't . . . Don't move!" He said.

"Kill it!" Alice demanded. "Don't just stand there, kill it!"

Bellowo's eyes hardened, and Augustus knew he was beyond his reach now. Again, he resented the lack of a mouth which he, at the moment, would use to call him a bloody idiot to his face.

The angry crowd reached them. They engulfed Bellowo in a tide of craggy, bearded faces and fiery eyes. Augustus stood up, turned around, and ran as fast as his new, alien legs let him.

Augustus watched the sun come up, and again, he noticed that he could not feel its warmth, same as he hadn't felt the grievous wounds that Ryerson and the others had inflicted upon him the night before. His state of physical numbness was only matched by that of his mind. He felt nothing. Was he becoming depressed? Maybe. Then again, his brain wasn't even human, so who could say? Maybe it was just a side effect of his new physiognomy.

On a positive note, he didn't feel any thirst or hunger either (and he had been wandering through the desert for hours). He wondered how long he would last in his current state. Did this body have some type of battery? It definitely didn't require any nutrients to keep functioning. Maybe there would be some kind of power outlet, somewhere back at the alien temple . . .

But was it worth it? Did he really want to live like that? Before he realized it, he was wandering again, this time, to the edge of the particularly steep mountain in which he had been hiding for the last (he calculated) two hours.

What if he jumped? Would the fall kill him, or would his new body simply recompose itself as it had been doing so far?

And what if it didn't? Was he ready to explore that final mystery?

He began climbing down the cliff. His body was, it seemed, on autopilot. Maybe it really boasted that feature, or maybe he was just acting on instinct. He didn't care anymore. Nothing really seemed to matter now. He just wanted to move, like a shark. Do something. Go somewhere.

He found himself wandering back to the camp. He climbed one of the low hills surrounding it and observed how a bunch of natives busied themselves rebuilding what he had unwittingly destroyed the night before. The armed patrols had doubled, making it impossible to infiltrate, at least during daytime. Not that he cared now.

A black spot in the corner of his eye drew his attention. It was a column of smoke. He creeped to the eastern brink and saw they were burning something. He already knew what it was.

They were cremating him, probably according to some local rite involving the victims of the "soul-stealing sand demon". A native priest was chanting while his remains burned atop a makeshift pallet. He watched Bellowo comfort Alice, first putting his arm around her shoulders, then kissing her.

Just as it had happened the night before during his fight with Ryerson, something clicked inside his head. It wasn't that he was attracted to Alice. He wasn't. But somehow, seeing the two together reminded him of what he had lost. That would never happen for him now. Not with Alice, nor with anyone.

Suddenly, his numbness disappeared and he felt as if he had been submerged in ice cold water. Again, a silent scream filled his mind.

The guard was sitting on the sand next to the burnt-out Ford. He was sucking on one of their exotic cigarettes, which, Augustus remembered, smelt vaguely like cinnamon. He crawled down the slope of the hill like a massive cockroach until his featureless face was right behind the guard's turban-clad head, and then he swiftly stabbed him with one of his blades. The guard let out a gush of cigarette smoke, then a gush of blood, and silently fell dead.

Augustus landed quietly right beside what was left of the Ford and crept inside it, then into the temple through the hole he had opened in its roof.

He didn't know what he was looking for, what he would find inside the bowels of the alien structure. He wasn't following any strategy. He simply knew that he was meant to be there. Down in the dark, with the dead things. And the rest of the monsters.

Ibai Canales hides somewhere in the cold mountains of Basque Country, in Northern Spain, from where he occasionally descends to wreak havoc upon the civilized world with the stories he writes and the graphic novels he draws.

DRY BONES

By Charles D. Shell

I would have never caught sight of the town if I'd been looking at the road ahead. It popped into view on the car's right when a gap opened in the tree line.

"Dwayne, stop!" I said, louder than necessary.

The blue-green Nissan Stanza screeched to a stop, catching gravel on the edge of the highway.

"What is it, baby?" Dwayne asked, worried.

Cursing came from the back seat. Fred had been asleep and the sudden stop put him on the floor.

"I'm okay. Just back up. I saw something."

Giving me an annoyed look, Dwayne backed up along the gravel until the town was revealed. I grinned.

"What the hell?" Fred said as he sat up and looked around.

"Tammy spotted another one," Dwayne said. "Don't ask me how."

I already had my smartphone out and looked at Google Maps. I frowned as nothing came up other than the road number. I did a little web search but so far as the internet was concerned, this place didn't exist.

"Whatcha got?" Dwayne asked. He shut off the engine and sat there, his arms crossed. His brown hair and angular face edged in sunlight, there remained a touch of annoyance.

"Sorry," I said. "Didn't mean to freak you out."

"I'm used to it."

I slapped him playfully.

"Turn the engine back on. It's too hot without the air conditioning," I said.

"Your constant air-conditioning is killing our gas mileage," Dwayne said.

My normal websites had nothing on this town. From the look of things, it must have been abandoned at least since the early nineteen-thirties. Probably too small to register.

"I got nothing. Slipped between the cracks."

"Want to check it out?"

I glanced at it again. It had one main street, partially covered with overgrown weeds, blown earth, and sand. A larger house sat on a small hill at the far end of the street, surrounded by what looked like sand dunes. It was an impressive structure. Must have been a mansion in Depression terms.

"Yeah. You think we can get down that road?"

"If not, there's enough area to turn around."

"Wonderful," Fred said. "Another dead town. I'm so excited." He dug around in the ice chest and pulled out a beer.

"Don't drink all the craft beer. I want to try some," I said.

"Firsties!" Fred said as he took a gulp.

"Pig."

Dwayne guided the Stanza down the cracked asphalt with care. I took the time to check my makeup and clothing, not that anyone but Dwayne would notice, but I wanted to look good in the photographs.

"Always good to be presentable in the dead town," Fred said.

I ignored him and ran a brush through my dirty blonde hair.

The main street wasn't as bad as it had looked from a distance. Despite a couple of scraggly trees pushing up between the cracks, it was mostly just a fine dusting of weeds. Even the Stanza could pass over it. I noticed the plants sprouting from the road were brown and sickly, perhaps from disease or lack of water. As if to reinforce it, a faded sign read: *Drought Warning* alongside the entrance into the town proper. Dwayne pulled up next to the general store at the corner and we got out to take a look.

A dry, dust-laden wind met us, dragging the moisture from my lips and eyes. It elicited a cough from me. The sound of the cough in the deserted town was somehow alarming—like talking in church.

Dwayne handed me a bottled water. I took a sip gratefully.

"Thanks."

"Careful with this grit in the air."

"All we are is dust in the wind," I said. He gave me a pained look.

"I guess we can see why this town was abandoned," Fred said, getting out of the car and stretching. He was a smaller, dark-haired man with a wiry build. "It's a shithole."

I looked around at the Depression-Era architecture. Despite the neglect, the buildings didn't look to be in that bad a shape. I pulled out my digital camera and started photographing everything. The general store's main windows were somehow still in one piece, even if filthy. The grime obscured whatever lay within.

"I'm going to check down towards the highway," Fred said.

"For what?" Dwayne asked.

"A good place to piss and maybe buried treasure."

"This is Depression Era. The only treasure you're liable to find is rusty signs," I said as I swung the camera around the street corner. An ancient stop sign sat there, barely legible. At a second glance, I realized there was something scratched on the surface of the sign. I zoomed in and read the words.

It thirsts.

I frowned and lowered the camera. I walked over to the sign and touched its weathered surface. Blowing sand and grit had left it smooth as glass, except for the words carved jaggedly into its surface, perhaps with a nail or knife.

"It thirsts," I said to myself. I jumped a moment later when Dwayne grabbed me around the waist.

"Sorry. Wasn't trying to scare you. What the hell does that mean? 'It thirsts?'"

"No idea."

"Sounds like a bad eighties horror flick."

I looked left and right at the two roads that formed the T shape at the end of the main street. My eyes lighted on a rusty Jeep. I walked over to it.

"That's not Depression Era. Looks like a model from the 1990s," Dwayne said as he opened the vehicle door. A stream of sand and dust poured out, along with the ragged remains of some clothing. The black leather seats were cracked and desiccated.

"Careful! Who knows what might nest in there!" Fred said as he came around the corner with a beer. "Might be snakes."

I involuntarily took a step back. I wasn't terrified of snakes, but I could do without any closer meetings. Fred handed me a beer. I took it without thinking. The cheery craft beer logo on its label had a grinning moose. Tasted pretty good, though.

"That's weird, huh? Just sitting here in the middle of nowhere?" Fred said.

"Yeah. Must have died and the owner didn't consider it worth it to tow. It's sure a good place to leave a vehicle if you don't want it found."

"The tags are still on it," I said.

"She's right," Fred said. "New Mexico plates, but I can't read the date on the tags."

"Huh," Dwayne said. His face got that blank look it always got when he thought deeply or worried. "I'll write it down and we can pass it along to the next cop we see. Just in case."

I looked at the now-sinister Jeep. I glanced in the back but didn't see any contraband or bodies. Fred reached in and pulled a set of keys out of the ignition.

"Left the keys, too."

"Any chance anyone lives around here?" I asked, feeling foolish even as I did. The Jeep was filled with dust and sand and looked as though it had sat there for a decade.

"If anyone's here, I'd guess the Adams Family house up there," Fred said, pointing at the large house on the hill. It was partially obscured by sand dunes.

"We can check for Morticia, but I doubt it," Dwayne said. "Place looks just as dead as the rest of the town."

I walked over to the general store and tried the front door. It came open with ease, a puff of stale, arid air blowing out. A smell like sawdust and faint corruption hit my nose. Despite the grime on the windows, they supplied enough light to see inside. A table sat in the middle of the floor, dust surrounding it. The countertop had a similar coating. Metal signs advertising coffee and medical cures hung on the walls, coated in rust. Another faded sign said: *Conserve Water. Remember the Drought.*

I took several pictures and even turned on the video function to get some footage. Only after I walked around the deserted store once did I see the markings on the floor. My own footprints were visible, but another set of footprints also showed up. It looked like a set of male shoes moving across the floor before it turned into a sloppy mess of smeared handprints and drag marks. It led to a large pile of dust in the corner. Something about the marks on the floor disquieted me, although I couldn't put my finger on why.

"Find anything?" Dwayne asked, making me jump a little.

"Look at that," I said. "Those haven't been here since The Depression."

"Probably another oddball tourist like us."

"Maybe," I said. I walked over to the pile of dust and kicked it apart. Beneath lay a pile of clothes. I picked it up and saw that it was a plaid shirt and jeans.

"Maybe the man came in and got naked."

Dwayne shrugged. His face had that blank look again. I didn't like seeing it. Underneath the shirt and jeans lay a pair of Nike shoes. I picked one up and looked at the tread pattern. It looked an awful lot like those treads in the dust.

"Where are the tracks back out?" I asked.

Dwayne looked around.

"I don't . . . I don't see them."

I slung my camera around my arm.

"Okay, I think this is creepy enough for me. Let's get out of here."

Dwayne didn't argue and we went back outside. Flying dust and grit greeted us.

"Where's Fred?" I asked.

Dwayne pointed at the large house.

"He wanted to check it out."

For an instant, I opened my mouth to say we should leave him, before simply cursing. Fred annoyed me from time to time, but I wasn't going to leave him in some abandoned town because of some vague fears. Besides, we could see the main highway from here. Hell, we could walk up there in fifteen minutes if anything went wrong. I still had a strong charge on my cellphone and it looked as though Verizon got reception even here. We were okay. This wasn't some teen horror movie.

"Let's go get him. But let's take the car. I don't feel like walking that far."

We jumped in the Stanza and slowly drove past the T intersection and swung around to the right. Part of me glanced back to make sure we could still see the main highway. It became obscured for a few minutes, until we turned up the small drive to the house, and then reappeared. I let out my breath in relief. Just seeing that road felt better. My mouth was too dry for more beer, so I grabbed a water bottle and drank that instead.

"There aren't any living plants in the town," Dwayne said. "But look around it."

I panned my eyes where he gestured. Green, healthy woods surrounded us, but I couldn't see a single green shoot inside the town limits.

"Some kind of toxic spill?" I asked, swallowing another mouthful of water. I was suddenly very thirsty.

"Dunno. Let's get out of here, anyway."

Again, I didn't argue. We pulled up alongside the oddly regular sand dunes that spilled around the side of the house. There was just enough space for the Stanza to park. We got out and looked around.

"Fred! Where the hell are you?!" Dwayne shouted.

I winced. Again, the noise in the silence of the town filled me with dread, although I couldn't have said why. He shouted again and again, but Fred didn't respond.

"Where is that little prick? Looking for treasure?"

The front door to the house lay wide open. Fresh tracks lay in the dust and grit. They led into the house.

"Goddamn it," Dwayne muttered. He reached underneath the car seat and pulled out a flashlight. "Stay here, I'm going to find him."

"The fuck I will! I'm not staying here by myself!" I moved to his side.

"Nothing's going to happen. It's a deserted town."

"Then nothing will happen if I go with you," I said.

Frowning, but unable to stop me, he just nodded and headed into the house. The Maglite beam cut through the gloom of the old house, revealing faded, but surprisingly-intact carpeting and furniture. Nothing much even looked out of place. If it wasn't for the layer of dust coating everything, I might have thought someone still lived here. The furniture wasn't even knocked over or damaged. A glass kerosene lamp sat on the hall table, obscured by dust, but in one piece.

"Christ, it doesn't look like anyone's been in here for eighty or ninety years," Dwayne, muttered as the flashlight beam panned around. A single set of footprints showed on the dusty rug. They headed down the corridor, past the stairs.

"Is it safe? Will the floor collapse?" I asked, my throat dry again. I took another sip of water. A few droplets fell into the dust and were immediately absorbed. The floor sucked them up.

It thirsts.

"It didn't collapse for Fred. Fred! What the hell are you doing?!" he shouted, his voice obscenely loud in the small space.

"Don't shout so much," I said.

"How else is he going to hear me?" Dwayne said.

Part of me wondered what else might hear him, but I pushed that thought deep down inside myself. That kind of thinking wasn't helpful or rational. That's what I kept telling myself.

We followed the footprints past a parlor clad in a century's worth of dust and into a kitchen straight out of an antique dealer's dream. Brick ovens and an iron-bellied stove dominated the room, along with an oak table. Antique chairs sat next to it. Fred's footprints moved around the room and out again. There were smeared handprints on the table and a drawer.

"Fred!" Dwayne shouted again. "I swear to fucking God, if you don't answer me, I'm going to leave your ass here!"

Nothing except the sound of wind sliding against the house. The sounds were magnified, perhaps. A storm?

Dwayne followed the footprints with a stream of obscenities. They moved into a dining room, only they looked sloppy and smudged, as if Fred had stumbled. Smeared handprints showed on the dining room tables and cabinets.

"What's that asshole doing?" Dwayne asked, smearing his hand across the handprints. A moment later, he let out a cry of pain and pulled his hand away as though the surface was red hot.

"Dwayne? What's the matter?"

"I don't know." He looked at the palm of his hand.

"Splinter?"

"No, I . . . don't know."

I looked at his hand. Where he'd touched the wood, it was cracked like a dry lake bed. Droplets of blood welled up from the cracks.

"Jesus!" I pulled out a tissue from my pocket and held it over the wound. Droplets of blood fell to the dust, where they disappeared in seconds. I looked over at where he'd touched the cabinet. There were a couple of fading spots, as if his blood seeped into the dusty wood. I swallowed, my throat suddenly like the Sahara. All of me felt like the Sahara.

"Let me try something," I said.

"How about not?" he said.

Morbid curiosity, however, drove me to put the tip of my index finger against the dust-covered wood. A sharp pain caused me to withdraw with a faint sucking sound. My finger looked like his hand. A droplet of blood welled up from the cracked surface. The residue on the cabinet disappeared before I could be sure it was even there.

"There's a chemical spill or something," I said, not sounding convincing to even myself.

"Fred!" Dwayne shouted. The fear in his voice eclipsed the anger for the first time.

"We should leave," I said.

"We can't leave him here, baby."

Several arguments against that warred in my head, but I knew he was right. My every instinct, however, screamed at me to get out of the house. Not just the house—the dusty, dead town. The thirsty town.

"Well then let's hurry the fuck up," I said, not liking the tinge of hysteria in my voice.

We followed the smeared foot and handprints along the floor and into the rear room. Sitting room? I didn't know enough about older houses to say. There was a couch and loveseat illuminated by the diffuse light coming from the dirty windows. Must have been some cracks in the windows, because the dust sat twice as deep in here. Drifts of dust filled the corners. The winds battered the old panes with angry insistence.

The flashlight beam revealed Fred, sitting on the loveseat.

I opened my mouth to say something when my throat closed up and an incoherent choking sound came out. A similar sound came from Dwayne.

Fred's skin wrinkled and cracked as we watched. The streams of blood ran down his face to the dust covering both him and the chair. His face became shrunken and wizened as it cracked, and even his staring, horrified eyes turned leathery and collapsed. The only sounds were the winds, the shifting of dust and a dry croak from Fred's shrinking throat.

Dwayne finally broke the paralysis. He turned to me and shouted: "Get the hell out of here!"

Needing no further encouragement, I turned and ran back towards the front. The howling of the wind doubled in volume.

I got no further than a dozen steps before the flashlight beam went wild and I couldn't see to run. I stumbled and fell onto the floor, which burned as terribly as the cabinet had. I let out a whimpering scream as my skin cracked and broke open wherever it touched anything. Fear drove me to my feet and I turned to see what had happened to Dwayne's flashlight. I lay on the ground next to the dining room table, so I snatched it up in my bloody hands and pointed it back towards Dwayne.

The dust had him.

Tentacles of dust engulfed him from the corners of the room, sliding up his legs and beneath his pants. Wherever it touched, the skin cracked and bled, the dust sucking greedily at the moist liquid. Dwayne's face was pale with horror and shock and he struggled to pull free, but it pulled the strength and vitality from him.

We locked eyes.

"Run!" he said.

I stood there, frozen.

"Run!" he said again. A single tear rolled out of his eye, only to be immediately absorbed. He tried to open his mouth to say it a third time—or maybe to only say goodbye—when tendrils of dust drove down his throat and he fell back into the thrashing dust.

The spell broke and I ran towards the front door with manic speed. I nearly fell three times, as the dust coating the floor became slippery and undulated. I had to grab a chair and a door to stop from falling, every touch burning me. The door remained mercifully open and I ran out of it into the swirling windstorm. It felt like no storm I had ever been in before. It didn't feel as if a wind drove the dirt and grit, but as if the dirt and grit flew around with angry malevolence, heedless of wind currents. It burned at my eyes and I could barely see anything. I stumbled around for a few minutes before I caught a glimpse of blue-green paint. The Stanza sat where we had left it.

Staggering in pain and shock, I pulled open the driver's side door—thankful we hadn't locked it—leapt in and shut the door behind me. The dust and grit surrounded the car, battering and shaking it. Catching my breath, I looked to the right of the car at the sand dunes.

They were being partially uncovered by the dust storm. Under each one, the dull gleam of automotive glass and steel appeared. Dozens of vehicles, buried under the sand. Like husks discarded from a spider's web.

"*OhJesusohJesusohJesus!* . . ." I repeated, over and over, until I realized that Dwayne had been driving. I nearly screamed at that knowledge before I remembered I had a set of spare keys in my purse. I reached in the back seat, fumbling through clothes and bottles. My blood smeared over everything until my fingers closed on the leather of my purse. I yanked it open, dumped everything on the front seat and grabbed my set of car keys.

The Stanza rocked from the force of the dust outside. The shocks creaked ominously.

I shoved the keys into the ignition and cranked. A plaintive wailing came from the starter. It cranked and cranked, but didn't want to turn over.

"*OhJesusohJesusohJesus!* . . ." I said, over and over. I'd never been particularly religious, but this seemed like an appropriate time to start. I caught sight of the highway we'd just left. I could see the goddamn highway. This couldn't be happening. It was *right there*. Things like this don't happen next to a major highway. Things like this *don't happen.*

Only they were.

The starter cranked for a long time, sounding slightly weaker—or maybe it was just my fevered imagination.

"Battery's dry!" I said and laughed hysterically. "Dry battery! Dry bones! 'Dem bones!"

The engine jumped to life. I let out a whoop of triumph for a split-second until I realized I left the air conditioner on. My hand leapt to the controls, but too slowly. The sand, dust, and grit shot out of the air conditioner vents and drove into my face. I opened my mouth to scream, but the dust drove down my throat and nose. I couldn't make a sound as it entered me and drank. I flailed around frantically, but not for long. It was very thirsty.

It thirsts.

Charles D. Shell is one of the winners of the Neoglyphic Entertainment Short Story Competition with his story "Boneyard Prophet." He also came in 2nd Place in the lulu.com short story competition for his story "Grass" and been previously published by A First Salvo Comic for Contract and Contract Solo Missions: Panzer. Several of his self-published novels are available on Amazon, including *Blood Calls*, *Mettle's Forge*, *Fourfold* and *Oath's Journey*. He lives quietly in Roanoke, VA, where he enjoys pen and paper RPGs, creates freelance artwork and waits for the transhuman singularity.

THE NOCTURNE OF MANIGAULT

By Joanna Costello

I never intended to return to this place. I wanted to stay away from it for as long as I was able. But the ties that are created in the course of one's life will reach you despite the distance or time placed between. With age, we come to understand how memories are revived by familiar things or places—in my case it was the mists that settled over rolling hills. Heavy mists which soaked the grass and wooden posts of barbed cattle fences along the train track. I had worked hard at suppressing these memories. The sky ahead looked dreary and the outline of a great forest could now be seen. Its immensity and denseness made me shudder. I diverted my attention to the letter I held in my hand. The letter was worn and riddled with illegible postage stamps. It was a testament to my nomadic life as a writer and a recluse.

I sought out large cities and relished in the anonymity it offered me. I wanted most of all to vanish from the reach of those who insisted in keeping in touch with me. It took too much emotional effort on my part to maintain friendships and intimate relationships. Despite purposefully placed obstacles, the letter I held survived the complications of the postal service's search for me. I was intrigued by the great deal of trouble the sender had gone through to find me and decided to read the letter straight away. I sat down at my writing desk with a cup of tea and opened the letter. I expected to be scolded for not keeping in touch than informed of the latest news from wherever it was I last moved from. I found that the letter was quite different and read as follows:

Jude,
Come back to me.
Yours,
Ramona

In the few moments it took for me to read the letter, my worst fears had been realized. I had spent years attempting to bury my past. Now these fears were back with a fierce vengeance. I felt tears of frustration welling up. My instinct told me to run. I put the letter down on the desk and found myself preparing to flee out of habit. I headed for my closet to find my suitcase as I had done so many times before. Something made me stop midway to place the suitcase on the floor. For the first time, I found myself evaluating my actions. I felt conflicted about running. Seeing her handwriting struck a resounding emotional chord within me. The graceful flourish of ink across the page in her familiar hand was the closest I had been to her for many years.

I had never known a moment's peace. Ramona is the closest I had come to anything like peace. It is because of her that I am able to enjoy early morning serenity, feel the mystical luminescence of the moon on my skin unafraid, or breathe the ocean's breeze in deeply and know eternity. Her selflessness was the reason I was free. I recalled the last words she whispered to me before I left. *"Jude, I want you to seek a life full of happiness and success. Go! I know you will return for me one day."* Freedom was granted through the actions of another person. I could pretend I never received the letter, rip it to pieces, or even burn it. I wasn't capable of doing that. My love and appreciation for her was etched into the very marrow of my bones and I would never be able to forgive myself if I ignored her request. So, I found myself on a train back to a place I had tried to lock deep down inside. My body spasmed with resistance, my teeth clenched down tight, and my jaw ached with determination all simply to stay put in my seat. I was heading to the place I had almost managed to convince myself never existed.

The train continued on through the abyss for what seemed like hours before beginning to slow its pace. Passengers looked around with apprehension sensing the change in the train's speed and realizing we were coming to a halt in the very heart of the forest. There were still another thirty miles until the next noted town. A glance out the window revealed a small, solitary, moss-covered platform built upon rock and brick—on it sat a single stone bench. The platform appeared ancient and completely isolated.

As I gathered my things I met the gaze of an older woman. A look of motherly concern flickered across her face as she watched a slender young man proceed to the door with a look of great resignation. I kept my head bowed as I exited the train to avoid the stares of the puzzled and curious passengers. I heard whispers of "haunted woods" behind me so I pulled my coat up around my neck as if to shield myself from their words. The train began to move and the passengers got their last look of the mysterious dark-haired man in the black winter coat.

I made my way down the platform steps and onto the pine needles that carpeted the forest floor. The whole scene was just as hauntingly beautiful as I remembered it. Majestic snowcapped mountains towered in the distance. Light from above fought its way through the high canopy creating an eerie effect upon the forest below. There was no sound, just the rise and fall of my own breath. I followed the path to the mountain hollow purely by memory. The forest was preparing for the arrival of winter but the map in my mind was of the forest in spring. I followed the cheery watercolor that revealed itself out of the rolling clouds of my memory. I imagined walking dirt paths dotted by quilts of little purple, pink, and yellow flowers. It was a cheerful distraction from reality and the blanket of dead, sodden leaves I presently trudged through. I felt the rays of sun warming my body and the frost-nipped tips of my fingers and could almost taste spring in the air but my reverie was interrupted by a break in the trees. I had reached the road to town which lay under a layer of sleet.

My jacket and belongings were quickly soaked since emerging from the forest's canopy of cedar and pine. The houses that occupied the area were in disrepair. Most were dilapidated—a few were now ruins conquered by Mother Nature. The door to one of the houses creaked open and a decrepit man with a few greasy strands of hair scratched himself, watching me as I passed. The man looked unhealthy and pale. Although his appearance did not reveal old age, his stance was un-steadied and he had a crook in his back. Dirt and ferns grew on the roof of his rotting house which bowed under its weight. He flashed me a crooked scowl and I glimpsed his yellowing teeth. He turned and disappeared back into his house closing the door behind him. I did not recognize him.

Each adjunct dirt road cut into the mountain's hollows and surrounding pine forest. Aside from tales and rumors of the diabolical, it was easy to see why many souls went missing here. Even though the hollows were once my childhood home, I still had difficulty distinguishing one road from the other. I managed to find my way as I made out the knot midway up a gnarled black tree that resembled a grotesque wailing woman. This was my road, Manigault Lane. A flutter of anxiety overcame me while gazing down the lane. Sodden trees were hunched over a dismal and dark road riddled with puddles and a wispy fog. Tall grass grew high on either side. Had my Ramona remained here on this hopeless road?

I hung my head with this sad realization and continued down the road staring at the ground. I had almost passed Mrs. Pettigrew's yellow house. I admired the ornate white trim around it as a child. It was the prettiest house in the spring. The old woman toiled tirelessly over her garden. Bunches of flowers would line the cobblestone path to her home. Edible violas and nasturtiums decorated the pastries and cakes she baked for my family. It was difficult to distinguish the shell of the once elegant folk home against the black backdrop of the dense pine forest. The house was rotting away. Its once shuttered windows had been smashed out. Trees now grew out of them like a parasitic foe tearing through the flesh of a conquered host. Amidst the overgrown yard, the bushes and shrubs that she had planted now seemed offensive. I hoped their doting caretaker Mrs. Pettigrew had met a better fate than her home now ravaged by the wild.

I examined the rest of the road and observed that the houses of our former neighbors were also abandoned. Judging by the state of their decay they had been evacuated long ago. Wooden frames of houses dampened by the hollow's ceaseless mists had succumbed to their own weight and fallen into the tall grass. Heaps of mossy lumber and crumbling brick remained proof that Manigault Lane had once seen more cheerful days. It was now an isolated and alien place reclaimed by the fauna of the ominous hollow. The whispers of "haunted woods" and "godforsaken" from the train made their way back into my thoughts and I began to feel vulnerable once again. The feeling I had worked so hard to overcome was creeping up my spine. I felt I was being watched. I did my best not to acknowledge the dreadful paranoia but my surroundings fueled my fear. Half expecting a demon to be following me, I snapped my head around like a feral dog and snarled "NO!" My lip curled and my teeth were exposed. But the road behind me showed no signs of life. It was silent and the fog began to thicken as it did when darkness began its descent over the woods.

I continued down the road. Icy splashes of water began soaking the bottoms of my trousers so I hastened my pace. As I got closer I could make out the ridge of the roof belonging to the Farmhouse where I had spent my childhood days. My heart sank at the sight of the house which was badly in need of repair. Its roof was riddled with loose shingles and forest debris. The once manicured lawn was a bed of pine needles and leaves the same as the woodland floor. The windows of the attic and the entire second floor were boarded up. A part of the front porch had caved in. The scene caused me to panic and I hurried past the ruins of what once was a white picket fence calling out for my sister.

"Go away!" A female let out a wild wail from inside. "Let me be! Please!" She began to sob. I tore open the door to find a frail and malnourished woman in a nightgown struggling to brandish the hot poker she had been using to tend to the hearth. She was wrapped in an old knitted quilt that I remembered covered my older sister and I as children in the bed that we shared. She was sallow, skin and bone, and her eyes were already sinking into the darkened hollows above her cheek bones. Her long raven hair pinned up into a wild knot on the top of her head. Despite her decline in health, her dark features remained as striking and mysterious as ever.

"*Ramona.*" I gasped horrified by what had become of my beloved sister. I placed my hand on my chest as if gesturing to a savage encountered in the wild. "It's me, Jude." Her dark eyes widened and the poker went crashing to the floor as her strength gave out.

"Jude!" She cried and fell. I snatched up the hot poker, placing it back on the hearth, and picked Ramona up off of the floor. She was feeble and tiny. I was able to carry her in my chest like a small child. She clung to my jacket sobbing in my arms. I sat on a wooden chair next to the hearth and rocked her gently. "What have they done to you?" I held back my tears as I rocked her. I had to remain steadfast for her as she had done for me long ago. "I'm so tired, Jude." She sighed and fell fast asleep still clinging to my coat. I sat grief-stricken for hours hoping that Ramona's state was due to her health and nothing else. The darkness of night had almost completely swallowed the purple twilight above the tree tops and I grew anxious. Ramona had kept up the kitchen and hearth. The rest of the house was covered in dust and cobwebs. Strangely, the only windows that remained intact were downstairs.

I wondered what became of our parents. Ramona had stayed behind to care for them and convince them to flee, to her own detriment. I was the youngest child and only son. Needless to say, I possessed a sense of entitlement which turned me into a selfish and rebellious individual. I tried to convince her to run away with me, claiming it would be our great escape. We could run from the fiends that robbed us of our sleep and sanity. Ramona refused, saying she could never dream of being so reckless. Instead, she did for our mother and father what they could not do for us—she stayed to watch over them. As I neared middle age, the regard in which I held my parents grew complicated. I bore resentment towards their inadequacies as parents and protectors. They were cowards for succumbing to the tormentors by which their children suffered so long. In the course of judging my own parents, I was forced to acknowledge my own faults. I had deserted my family, a guilt I had borne for many years. I turned my back on my sister who had sacrificed her own happiness to carry a weight so great it had now broken her physically, maybe mentally as well. My way of coping with anything that tested my resolve or courage was to avoid it. My intentional absence robbed me of being able to save my family from whatever was afflicting them. Perhaps discovering my sister like this was my divine punishment.

I did not speak ill of our parents in front of Ramona as filling her head with regret and sadness might prove counterproductive. I was determined to get her out of here. This meant that Ramona needed to be fed, rested, and in better spirits before making the trek back up Manigault Lane and out of the hollow. I would sprint the length of the lane with her on my back if I had to but she would still need to be well enough to hold on.

Then quickly, in the window, I witnessed the outline of a person's head, neck, and shoulders. It flickered and then faded against the moonlit forest in the background. It had been watching me. Fear melted over me, gluing me to my seat. "*This is not happening,*" I thought. I decided that the most adult thing I could do was appear stoic in the face of the startling phenomenon. I had denied it for years but the phantom I had just seen and its counterparts shaped me into the eremitic and paranoid man that I am today. With age, you expect to be able to reason your childhood phobias away with your newfound understanding of the physical world. Here I sit, cradling Ramona in my arms, still struggling to come up with an explanation.

This first sighting of the shadowy specter had confirmed the one and only longtime truth I held. It confirmed my belief that Earth remains an unknown, unpredictable, and unsafe place. I had lost faith in the abilities of modern scientists and academics after spending hours perusing university libraries. In their research, I discovered a discreetly prejudiced language required to maintain well-defined and self-created laws of science. They had lost the creative and exploratory essence required to identify the incomprehensible, from which all scientific exploits are inadvertently born. These professionals, who consider themselves progressives, had created their own boxed thinking. My attempts to appeal to various researchers to reconsider of my requests for assistance with scientific study were met with contempt. My paranoia as an adult had become debilitating without the reassurance that my phenomenal experiences could be policed by science at least. After being haunted by shadows that are not cast by any explainable person or object for many years, I am now afraid of my own. I believe, developmentally, I will remain a trembling little boy without the answers I so desperately seek.

Time wore on and the midnight hour came and went as I kept silent vigil over Ramona. I watched what I could only describe as black figures materializing before my eyes. Each shadow that appeared exposed itself to me intentionally and then, for reasons unknown, would fade away. I had seen this behavior before. Although the phenomenon was brief, these visual incidents were burned into my memory. It became a compulsion to fixate on them and play them over and over again in my mind, frightening myself more than necessary. They were the cause of many sleepless nights. What I saw now felt calculated and as if these entities had amassed power during my long absence.

As a child, I remember being startled out of a deep sleep to the terror-filled sensation of being watched. I would strain my eyes to identify the cause for alarm. In the dark I could make out the familiar shapes and shadows of my bedroom. "There's mother's rocking chair and that's a table," I whispered the way a frightened child does when trying its best to be brave. But then I would see something in the corner of the room and remark that it was independent of both the floor and the ceiling. There would be no visible flutter of wings or sound ruling out animals. The dark form remained still, suspended in air, and it was always too high to be a shadow casted by any object in the room. It would grow larger and larger and I would watch in horror as it extended itself downward and outward in a pulsating movement. A creature of shadows struggling to manifest in front of the child it craved to torture, to possess, to consume. The figure was never successful, exhausting itself into a wisp and vanishing into the night, its purpose still a mystery.

Ramona stirred, bringing me back to the present. Her purple-veined eyelids fluttered, exposing the whites of her eyes. The bottoms of her irises rolled toward the back of her head. She was fighting her sleep and she groaned in an attempt to speak but succumbed to her exhaustion. In the window to my left, a tall dark figure stalked in an apelike manner across the edge of the property. Its appendages would separate and realign with the dark form of its body, indicating a swing of arms and stride of legs reminiscent of ancient Neanderthals. The dark oval shape which I took for his head was fixated in our direction throughout the time it remained in view through the window. I spotted movement in the corner of my eye. A shadow figure was descending the staircase. I lost sight of the ape man in the window. How many surrounded us? The stair case was cloaked in darkness, allowing the figure to get alarmingly close. Even in involuntary sleep, Ramona could sense the danger as her eyes fluttered wildly in an attempt to open them. The shadow on the stairs appeared unnaturally thin and moved in the creeping, rhythmic manner of a bobbing stick insect. The movements of its stilt-like limbs were slow and deliberate. It stopped on the lowest step that darkness would allow, seeming to avoid the reach of the lamps' illumination and began, what I could only describe as, a vile song. A string of breathy whispers whose end notes possessed a throaty base, "sphih sphah, sphih sphah," filled the kitchen. From outside, voices joined in at different intervals, speeds, and pitches, "sphih sphah, sphih sphah," growing louder and louder until whispers were coming from all around us. The noise had reached such a dizzying crescendo that I wanted to cover my ears. Soon, the echoing was unrelenting and I could no longer discern whether the sound came from all around me or from inside my own head. I wanted to claw at my face or viciously jam my fingers into my ears.

Ramona whimpered in her sleep so I cradled her tight as they continued to breathe their wretchedness onto us. All the while dark figures appeared and disappeared out of thin air outside. A horde of shadows, some flitting and others lumbering like unknown beasts, could be seen out of every window. Despite my fearful trembling, I did my best to keep my voice from reflecting the fear I felt as I spoke into my sister's ear. "I'm here. Jude is here. We're going to make it to the morning." It was the same chant we recited as children huddled together in bed. This was before our mother and father had encountered the phantasms which had eroded their physical and mental health.

I sat transfixed by the movement and sound all around me. The lack of sleep and the siege upon my senses felt violent and exhausting. I felt cornered, naked, and exposed as the silhouettes taking contorted human forms exposed themselves to me. My panic became paralyzing as the floor boards above creaked with the weightbearing of footsteps upstairs. I tried in vain to assure myself that there was no other physical being in the house despite not having visited the second floor and being sure. I now witnessed dust, disturbed by the creaking floor boards, swirling over my head. There was *someone* up there! I had never seen the shadow figures manifest into a physical form. But then again, I remembered a time when these ghostly beings were simple forms that could not emit sound, take any identifiable form, nor multiply.

I could not gauge the extent of their paranormal abilities. The ebb and flow of activity felt planned and the shadow man's eerie whispered ballad seemed to tear down all physical divides. Under the song's influence, all perception of my surroundings felt dangerously limitless. It was the kind of perception of the world that provoked grandiose thoughts unique to psychopaths or persons with a predisposition towards deviant behavior. It made me feel as if I was invincible or, at least, it wanted me to believe I was. Their voices penetrated my thoughts and with that my sound judgment. I felt my defenses tumbling down with every throaty note. My mind had become vulnerable.

The waves of terror I was forced to endure, like the relentless waves of the ocean crashing over me and receding, had left me weak and breathless. I wanted to come up for air. Was their intent to incite madness? Were there others, imprisoned or in asylums, who had gone through this? Did these creatures wish to weaken the minds of men and for what purpose? Once inside the mind, what becomes of the body or of the soul? The black specters moved in closer, some in abrupt jerking movements like insects and others with a labored step as if maimed. I pulled Ramona in tight, ready to embrace the wrath of a foe I did not know how to fight and wanted desperately to become a part of, for mercy's sake.

I looked up towards the heavens and released a crazed laugh. Mankind is a naïve race of beings. How could a civilization, knowing next to nothing of the great universe they live in, feel so arrogant and secure with their position in it? I now understood how the certainty of death, or our struggles to cope with the mysteries of the world we live in, drive people into a state of outright denial and fantasy. The need for security compels an entire alleged rational species of beings to dream up a fantastical tale of an all-knowing and powerful man in the sky who controls our destiny and could gift us everlasting life. We choose ignorance in defiance of truths we refuse to accept. What of the scientists or the authorities?

Why not torment those who disregard the extraordinary? Why torment us? "Maybe we all deserve to be obliterated. We're fools," I whispered, admiring the changing colors of the sky. The soft glows of purple, pink, and orange now smeared across the cosmos. "Morning!" I roared and reality came crashing over me.

I realized that the entity's song had literally caused divides to disappear. Whereas I had seconds ago been exposed to the natural world of earth and sky, I sat again in our house with the ceiling above me and its aged walls. To the left, the stick man on the stair case was fading back into the shadow before my very eyes. His uncanny melody forced to harmonize with the sounds of nature waking to greet the sun. The birds began singing in the trees and the sound of the morning winds rustled through the pines, drowning out the last of the shadow creatures' sounds. The dawn brought about renewed vigor and the certainty that I would not last another night.

That morning, I placed Ramona on the floor before the hearth so that she could get as much sleep as she could. I would have to wake her for the trek to town soon. I found some bread and cheese in the kitchen and put a kettle on for tea. Ramona slept until mid-morning. When she stirred I greeted her and showed her the plate of food waiting for her on the kitchen table. I wanted her to try to eat something. She stood up weakly from her sleeping position on the floor and shuffled over to the table. The quilt I found her in yesterday was still wrapped around her. "We've got to get to the train station in town. We can't afford to wait at the hollow's platform. I'm not sure how often the train stops," I explained as I scrambled to and fro, gathering her belongings and throwing them into my suitcase. "You'll only need a single change of clothes. We will have to get you new clothes in the city. These are threadbare!" I paused, holding the ratty dress I found up to Ramona. But she had not moved let alone touched her food. "Ramona, are you listening to me? You've got to eat." I watched Ramona gaze out of the window. She wore a glazed expression and nodded her head in rhythm as if hearing a faint song that I could not. "I apologize for insisting. I know you may not be hungry but you'll need your strength." She turned her gaze towards me and smiled endearingly.

"Oh Jude! I'm so glad you're here!" I smiled. She seemed unstable but in good spirits.

"So am I. After last night, I believe this visit has been long overdue. I never could have imagined that the situation had reached this magnitude. I want to know everything but it will have to wait for the train." I motioned to her breakfast. "Please, finish your breakfast so that you can change out of your nightdress." Her eyebrows furrowed in a look of confusion.

She shook her head in disbelief. "But Jude, you just got home. Where are we going?" I tried my best not to be impatient with Ramona. She was fragile after the routine violence subjected onto her by the nighttime terrors I had witnessed. Her mind was left tattered and frayed and her body undernourished. These terrors were the only explanation I could think of for her odd behavior and malnourishment. She behaved as if she had not heard a single word I had spoken.

"No, no. We can't stay here. It's too dangerous." But I had already lost her attention. Her gaze had turned towards the kitchen window, once again captivated by some invisible presence. "Come now, we must prepare to leave." I walked over to the table and assembled a piece of cheese and bread ready to feed her.

"No, Jude!" She swatted the food from my hand and onto the floor. "I'm not leaving! What I wanted was for *you* to be here with me . . . with us!" Ramona exclaimed. Her choice of words gave me a fright. There was nobody left in the house. What did she mean by *us*? Was it too late? Had she been permanently afflicted by these nightmarish fiends? "Oh no, please," I begged. "You're not making sense. It's just you and I left now. Father and Mother are dead." There was no time for eloquence. I had to be blunt. She needed to understand the urgency of the situation with which we were being faced.

"Our parents aren't dead!" she snorted. She reached for both my hands and cradled them as if explaining to a child that which is so obviously clear. "They're thriving. They have forgiven you and they want us all to be together." She patted my hand. "Now let's go put your things away upstairs in Mother and Father's room. I've already claimed our old room for my own," she teased.

"Ramona." I grew frustrated by the preposterousness of the conversation I was having with my older sister. We were wasting precious time. I wanted to demonstrate the impossibility of what she was saying. In the true essence of a younger sibling, I challenged her. "If our parents are alive, take me to them. I want to see them for myself."

Ramona reciprocated in the manner of an older sibling prepared for such a squabble; she confidently headed up the stairs and so I followed. The staircase was so rickety it forced me to pay close attention to each step. I observed that the stairs were covered by a thick layer of dust. On the second floor, there was even more dust and even small debris that had fallen from the decaying roof. However, all of the footprints belonged to the same person, Ramona. There were no other footprints to indicate that anyone else had been on the second floor but her. It was still and dark as all the windows had been boarded up. The entire second floor was veiled in darkness with very little light entering from the sun that shone outside. Had my father boarded up the windows and why?

Ramona, barefoot and still in her nightdress, led me into our parents' room which reeked of mildew and the unpleasant stench of fermented vegetation. I brushed thick cobwebs out of my hair as I crossed the threshold. Tiny translucent spiders skittered across the back of my neck. Ramona presented the room to me excitedly. The bed was made but appeared to have sat untouched for years. The covers were vermin-eaten, dank, and dusty. "You can't expect me to stay here. This room is uninhabitable." She appeared to be surprised by my remark, offended even. This prompted me to act with caution and I asked again slowly, "Where are mother and father?"

Sensing condescension, Ramona angrily spat, "*Ugh!* Here!" She turned on her heels and marched across the hall to our old bedroom. I coughed as all the commotion disturbed the dust on the floor. The lack of ventilation made it stuffy and hard to breathe. Again, the room was covered in grime, unused for many years. Spider webs blanketed every inch of furniture and ferns grew in pockets in the corners of the ceilings. She could not possibly be sleeping up here. My sister was crouched on the floor reaching for something under the bed and she emerged holding a large bundle wrapped in black fabric. She placed the bundle carefully on the bed. "See?"

I gasped in horror as she pulled the last bits of fabric away revealing the bundle's contents. There lay a pile of bones, the larger of which were arranged neatly to fit into the fabric. Smaller bones tumbled out onto the bed. The skull was missing. A putrid stench wafted up my nostrils, causing me to wretch in front of my smiling sister. I grabbed Ramona by her shoulders and shook her fiercely. "What have you done?" I screamed.

"Jude! Let go of me!" She was so feeble that my fierce grasp hurt her. She crumpled to the floor when I released her. "It's mother! It's mother!" she sobbed on the ground.

"This isn't our mother! This is a corpse, Ramona! What is the matter with you?"

"No! Father's here too! You must've seen them for yourself? Last night!" She shook her head at me in confusion. She was convinced that they were alive. "They were so pleased to have another person in the house. I just know they were up here visiting last night and I missed it because of this thing I'm trapped in!" Ramona pulled at the skin of her face resentfully.

I remembered hearing the footsteps and the floor boards above me creak amongst the whispers of the shadow beings. It was as if someone with physical weight were walking around. This realization must have shown on my face because Ramona nodded vigorously. "Yes! Yes! You see? You remember! And I've kept their bones nicely. Here's mother's and let me get father for you . . ."

"No! Ramona!" I yelled, snatching her by the arm before she could crouch under the bed again. "We're leaving!" I growled. She struggled against me like a child in the midst of a fit. I dragged her through the bedroom door and back towards the stair case. Out of the corner of my eye, wispy black smoke appeared in the air at the far end of the hall. It began moving in a swirling, circular motion, rapidly forming the beginnings of an orb. Ramona screamed obscenities at me. She kicked and spat, refusing to leave.

"No! Listen to me, you idiot! You're not listening to me!" she screeched. I scooped her up and threw her over my shoulder in one swift movement. A glance be-hind me, as I tore down the stairs away from the dark-ness of the second floor, revealed the two legs and torso of a shadow figure. *They can only manifest in darkness. Someone was helping them to materialize.* A pang of fear sent my heart racing as I realized the fiend was attempt-ing to take shape. On my way out, I picked up my suitcase in my free hand and stormed out of the house, slamming the door behind us. Ramona was screaming like a lunatic. She punched, clawed at my face, and tried to tear at my hair. "Listen to me!" she screamed. I threw her down in front of our crumbling picket fence.

"What, Ramona? What possible explanation could you have for what you've just shown me? What?" I roared.

Trembling from head to toe and sobbing, she be-gan in a tiny voice, "Jude, p-please. Don't leave, please. I took care of mother and father as best I could. I did eve-rything they asked." Genuine tears were streaming down her face. "When they grew too weak to get out of bed, I honored their wishes and stopped feeding them. At first, I refused to obey because I didn't understand what it meant to feel trapped within your own body. Remember the ghosts in our bedroom? Mother and father were able to communicate with them, Jude. Actual contact with the other side. It's unheard of! Haven't you ever wondered why we have not been able to unravel the mystery of life after death? It's because anyone who uncovers the mys-tery chooses death in the end!"

I grew weak and my knees gave out. I fell to the ground before my sister. I was going to be sick. Ramona, who was already on the ground, crawled towards me and continued her deranged rant. "I choose death. But they've requested another person to take my place when I have passed." Ramona smiled and stroked my cheek with her dirt-covered hand. "Now you must do for me what I've done for our beloved parents so that I can join them in the darkness from which everything is born. Look at me, Jude. It's only a matter of time before I die. I can feel the life draining from my body with every day that passes. Come with me, my dearest brother. With your wit, you could be the first to return and reveal to the nonbelievers the secrets of the chilling voices in the night, the things that inexplicably move, or being touched by something that isn't there. You must want answers or justice for what we've gone through, Jude." Disgusted, I rose from the ground. She grabbed my pant leg in a panic and began begging, "Please stay, Jude! You must prepare my body, keep my bones, and give my skull to . . ."

"No! I want both answers and justice but not enough to resort to sacrilege! What have these creatures done to you?" I hissed. I grabbed my sister's face and squeezed it so I could look into her eyes. Her expression appeared hurt, confused, and desperate as a child attempting to convince an adult of something they want more than anything in the world. I began to yell at her, hoping to be heard through her insanity. "You are a murderer. *You* made our mother and father ill by starving them to death. *You* made them suffer a cruel and inhumane death. *You* gave them a damnable departure into the afterlife."

"N-No. That's not. Please, Jude." She sputtered and threw herself at my feet, prostrating before me. Her display meant nothing to me. I continued.

"I will never forgive myself for deserting my family. I will never forgive you for murdering our mother and father." Tears now streamed freely down my face. My heart ached with the knowledge of my parents' grisly death at the hands of my maniacal sister. "And I'll never forgive myself for what I'm about to do now." The last bit was barely a whisper. Before I realized it, I was sprinting, suitcase tucked under my arm, back up Manigault Lane. My sister was still struggling after me. When I glanced back, Ramona had stumbled into the mud of the street, still calling my name.

I ran from the house until I had departed Manigault Lane. Before these events, I believed my trip home would prove a sort of spiritual pilgrimage. I wanted to wash myself clean of the wrongs I had committed in the embrace of my courageous caretaker and older sister. I had hoped to be presented to my elderly parents who would absolve me from the disappointment I had caused them. Most of all, I wanted to return to my home and dispel the supernatural legacy with a battery of amateur scientific theory. My intent was that my journey home would spur internal healing. With everything that had just transpired, I had never been so disappointed in my life. That I had ever dared to hold onto a glimmer of hope was humiliating.

I walked on for a few miles in the late afternoon sun up the main road to town. I would have preferred the solitude and bird song of the forest but could not risk waiting at the stone platform as dusk approached. I would rather die than live through another night in the godforsaken woods. I promised myself that this would be the last time I ever laid eyes on the hollow. I managed to bribe an old farmer passing with a horse and cart. At the sight of the money he reluctantly obliged although he eyed me with suspicion the whole way. He never attempted to engage me in conversation and I was grateful. Once we got into town, I thanked the stranger and considered seeking the help of the authorities. They always offered more ridicule than assistance whenever my parents had attempted to reach out to them. This of course was when the ghostly disturbances first occurred. Despite the entertainment they enjoyed at my parent's expense, they never stayed at our house past the afternoon hours. I wondered if any of those men remained to see the ruined state of the hollow and determine whether its desertion by others was in any way related to the foredoomed fate of my family. Was this a psychosis or was my family being manipulated by some unexplainable evil influence? I sat in the town's empty station contemplating all these things waiting for the last train to anywhere else. As twilight descended, once more I thought of Ramona. I thought about the nighttime world of specters that would be emerging to swallow her whole. They are out there among the trees, patiently waiting and coercing their next victim. Again, I have deserted Ramona. In doing so, I shall soon be just as guilty of murder as she.

Joanna Costello is a horror writer who favors dark poetry and short stories. In addition to Hinnom Magazine, her work has been featured by FunDead Publications out of Salem, Massachusetts. She is originally from Pāhoa, Hawaii.

NOTHING BUT DANS, ALL THE WAY DOWN

By Konstantine Paradias

"So that's it? You don't even care?" Lumberjack Dan asks from the living room, trans-dimensional goo still clinging on him. By the time I'm back from the kitchen, he's made himself cozy, picking ectoplasm off his plaid shirt.

"Watch out for Invisible Dan," I warn him. Lumberjack Dan hops onto his feet, searching for the slight sag on the couch, the depression that a pair of feet would make on the carpet. By the time I've come back, he's run around in circles, before plopping himself down.

"Watch it!" Invisible Dan shouts. I'm bringing in the nachos and salsa, when I catch the familiar rumble of Invisible Dan fumbling his way across the living room, searching for the edges of the dining table. The plates have come tumbling down and one of the paintings has been torn from the wall and trampled before Invisible Dan's rampage finally stops.

"Is he . . . is he going to be okay?" Lumberjack Dan says, head cocked to search for the sound of Invisible Dan stomping around.

"He's gonna be fine. He just can't see himself, so he's got trouble orienting. Science Dan promised to make him a pair of refracting light goggles to help with that, but he's been slacking," I say, before dipping a half-dozen nachos into the spicy mix.

"Then the rest have already got here before me?" Lumberjack Dan asks.

"Oh my, yes. There was Wizard Dan, Astronaut Dan, and Olympian Dan and Cyborg Dan, three Crime-fighter Dans, an Elf Dan, a Giant Hunter Dan, a Wolfman Dan, and a Vampire Dan. And then there was Just There Dan, but he didn't do much."

"Was there a Batman Dan?" Lumberjack Dan says, halfway through stuffing his face with a handful of nachos, salsa splattered all over his rugged beard.

"Well, duh," I say "tortured billionaire, gadgets, the works. Burst right through my garage, spouted some nonsense and ran for it. He was back, two weeks later. Turns out, his money isn't legal tender in this universe and police don't have any patience for masked avengers over here."

"But he did tell you, didn't he? Why he came all the way here?" Lumberjack Dan says, struggling with the cap on his beer bottle. I let him sweat for a while, before I finally help him twist it off.

"Something about a Grand Conjecture. Didn't pay too much attention, if I'm honest. Had my hands full trying to keep my landlord from kicking me out, what with my garage exploding and all that."

"It's called the Grand Conjunction, Dan. And we *need* you," Lumberjack Dan says somberly, before stuffing another handful of nachos into his face. "The Multiverse is in dire peril. The Anti-Dan is . . ."

"For Pete's sake, not you too! Why can't you weirdos get it, I'm *nobody*," I say, pushing myself out of my couch. Lumberjack Dan shoots up behind me, nachos and salsa firmly at hand.

"Then why do you think we all come here? Why do we all attempt this weird journey, across countless universes, trudging through . . . that thing," Lumberjack Dan says, pointing at the howling non-space above where my TV used to be, "only to find *you?*"

"I don't know, maybe I'm not your guy! Maybe I'm just Regular Dan, you ever think about that? Or maybe I'm just Roped Into This Dan, the guy with the job and the house and a girl named Mandy that gave up on his sorry behind and a dead end job. I could be No Hope Dan, how about that?" I say, gritting my teeth. Somewhere behind us, there's the sound of distant cursing and I know that Invisible Dan's trapped himself in the bathroom again.

"I've met No Hope Dan. He's just a hippie who's trying to make a living off cat videos. He still lives with his mother and even *he* answered the call," Lumberjack Dan rumbles, his salsa-dripping finger pointed accusingly. "A hundred thousand of us: Dans of every shape, size, and configuration, we've been gathered to face the coming storm."

"Then go! Save the multiverse! You guys got the talent, you got the numbers! What good could I possibly do?" I say, my voice teetering on the edge of hysteria. An evil cackle wafts up from the fruit cellar and I know it's NEET Dan, pausing in between his bouts of online trolling to savor my despair in between his regular schedule of raiding my fridge and not paying rent. Undaunted, Lumberjack Dan points his nacho-stained finger at me and booms:

"Every single Dan in the entirety of Creation isn't enough to take down the Anti-Dan and you know it. God knows we've tried it. We had Invincible Alien Dan and God Emperor Dan go up against him but he's sent us packing, every time. We've sent the entire Dan Fleet against him, but the defenses in his Universe are nearly impossible to break through. We need someone who can wield the power to destroy him, the power that runs through the quantum fabric of all reality like a raging wildfire, you know, that weird energy-energy stuff that they have in comic books but not in the real world, with all that Kirby crackle in it, the . . ."

"Please don't," I moan.

"We need the warrior-king of a million Universe . . ." Lumberjack Dan says, licking his fingers.

"No, no, no come on . . ."

"We need *Champion* Dan," Lumberjack Dan says and before I know it, I've waved my hand in that certain kind of way, it's like riding a bike, you never forget it no matter how hard you try, and a wave of energy-energy as big as a steam hammer hits Lumberjack Dan and sends him flying across the living room and into the hole in the Multiverse, back to whatever strange world he's come from.

"Not again," I moan. There's a crashing noise from the bathroom and I don't even have to look to know that Invisible Dan's torn down the medicine cabinet again.

"I got this, I got this!" I hear him shout and I just plop myself down on the couch and stare into the shimmering tear on the face of Creation and realize that I'm too tired to bother with dinner.

"God, I miss Michelin Chef Dan," I say, before reaching for the takeaway menu.

"Dark clouds gather. The end of all hope is at hand," Shaman Dan says, leaning back on my boss's swivel-chair.

"What have you done with Mister Murdoch?" I say, searching the darkened office for his squishy, pudgy form. Instead, I hear some muffled groan or another coming from the filing cabinet.

"The Murdoch man is in the broom closet, safe in the arms of Mescalito," Shaman Dan says, his bone-charms rattling across his caftan. "He shall not interfere in our discussion."

"This was supposed to be my performance review," I say. From across the desk, Shaman Dan nods sagely and passes me a glass of lukewarm coffee.

"I peered into the Murdoch's mind. His review was not favorable. You had really bungled up the last quarter," he says and a thousand hours of pointless overtime flash in my head and all the dirty looks from all the office cliques click together. I'm sipping at the bitter coffee that's gone cold and know how this review was supposed to have gone.

"I did what I could . . ." I mutter. The coffee tastes strange, leaving my mouth drier than ever before. Could be nerves. Has to be.

"You toiled under a halogen sun in a bleak place, doing menial work in a mundane Universe, all for nothing," Shaman Dan says. On his shoulder, something tiny and mean with an all-too-familiar face giggles evilly.

"God, I can't stand another job hunt . . ." I say, cringing at the thought of piles of complimentary biscuits and loan notices gathering under the rug.

"This would have been your sixth place of work?" Shaman Dan asks, pawing through the scattered stack of printouts all over Mister Murdoch's desk. Out from the shadows, the ghost-forms of wizened reptiles fix their amber gazes at me.

"Six different jobs in six years. I know it doesn't look good . . ." I say. Shaman Dan cuts me off with a wave of his hand.

"Your feet are cracked and dusty. Your hair is tousled by the whipping wind. Your back is peeling from destiny's glare," Shaman Dan says in a low growl. Around us, the air is so thick, you could almost cut it. Something bobs across the surface of the coffee, reaches up a tiny appendage and *waves* at me.

"What the heck is that supposed to mean?" I ask, confused. "What did you put in the coffee—"

"For too long, you have wandered in the wasteland of your life. For too long, you have put off the great turning of the wheel," Shaman Dan says and his breath is like the desert wind, grating against my skin.

"What are you doing? There's sand, why is there . . ."

"Ku'toom maa-ta, the drums are calling. Fa-toom kaa-toom, hear him stomping down the hill . . ." Shaman Dan says and there's a slight hint of an Irish accent in his voice like he's overcompensating and I want to say something, but his caftan starts to weave and bob and suddenly he explodes into bugs and I want to scream but I can't because they might fly into my mouth . . .

"Can I at least get my phone—"

I wake up in freefall, with a world of greens and ambers rising to meet me and the air whipping at me so hard it threatens to flay my skin off. There's a shadow across the sun, a rainbow glint from the corner of my eye and then talons grasp me in mid-air, stopping my descent.

Soon as my guts have plopped back into their proper place, I start to scream.

"Oi, keep it down," someone roars above me in a menacing baritone. I turn to look up at it and see my own face, covered in scales with two pairs of eyes and a grin made up of three rows of razor-sharp teeth.

I start to scream again and I don't stop, even after there's tiny lights dancing in my eyes, even after my throat's gone way past raw.

"Woden help us, it's been fifteen minutes," Dragon Dan says, "Do *something* about it, will you?"

"Hold my beer," I hear someone say and feel them shuffling behind me. I turn to look and only have time to catch a glimpse of a head full of flaxen hair that shine like the midday sun sticking out from under a horned helm before an arm the size of a tree trunk smashes into my face.

"We call it the Dan Hold," Industrialist Dan says, his hands sweeping majestically over the 360-degree panorama, revealing the sprawling metropolis of glinting spires and shimmering castles, the hanging hive-towns and floating neighborhoods that orbit the stone Dan-head, hewn from the dead cinder that once was a sun.

"Jesus wept, that's embarrassing," I say while trying not to stare too hard at the levitating gondolas that pass by the window. A crowd of Dans of every shape, size and configuration float by me, all too eager to check out the newcomer.

"The Anti-Dan draws closer by the minute," Adventurer Dan says, bringing up a complex hologram with a wave of his hand, "before long, he will have completely transmuted his home Universe into a Thaumic Resonator and then ..."

"You utter bastards," I groan as I check the back of my head, feeling the baseball-sized bump. "You kidnapped me."

"Kidnapped is a strong word," Fire Elemental Dan says, smokeless flame erupting from his steepled fingers. "We merely ... requisitioned you."

"You had that Shaman weirdo put something in my coffee and then you dropped me from the sky and then ..." I pause, noticing the jock in the horn helm staring at me from the other end of the table. "*That* dingbat tried to bust my head open!"

"Thunder God Dan didn't mean to hurt you," Femme Fatale Dan says and I stare up at her hourglass figure and skintight attire, an unpleasant tingle running down my spine. "Isn't that right?"

"You were screaming like a little girl. For fifteen minutes," Thunder God Dan offers and, all across the room, the Dans shrug and nod, impressed. Android Dan, his silvery uniform seeming to somehow dance in the light, says:

"We would never have done this against your consent. But the situation is dire. Universe 6-Omega ..."

"The Anti-Dan Universe," Wizard Dan butts in. Android Dan shoots him a dirty look. When Wizard Dan has shriveled into his chair, he adds:

"The Anti-Dan Universe has gone through a series of changes. Apparently, the Anti-Dan has abandoned his original plan of gradually eliminating all Dans from every possible Universe. It seems that the sheer number of realities make killing every one of us individually logistically impossible. And so, he has constructed a doomsday machine..."

"Thaumic Resonator," Adventurer Dan says. Android Dan shoots him a smoking glare, followed by, literally, a thrown punch—his clenched fist blasts off from his extended wrist, propelled on miniature jets at supersonic speed. It smashes into Adventurer Dan's gaping jaw, knocking him out cold. When the rocketing fist has orbited back to the empty wrist and locked snugly back into place, Android Dan says:

"Which will allow him to generate a Null cloud that will eliminate the entirety of the Multiverse and every Dan that has ever been or ever will be in the process. So far, we have been unable to breach his defenses and every confrontation has resulted in abject failure. Should he succeed, then it will be the end of life in the totality of existence. Please, Dan, you are the only one who can stand up to him. You are the Champion Dan."

Across the hall, all around the glass dome, in screens all across the city, the Dans of every conceivable reality are staring at me, waiting with bated breath and I know it's easy to make all of this come to an end; all I have to do is say 'no' and stomp out of there. I want to kick down their table and tear down their idiotic Dan Hold; I want to tear that stupid face from the Universe and I want to never have to see any of those sad weirdos ever again but I know they'll never let me go.

Not until it's done.

"Okay," I say, and the Dans break into a deafening cheer and Femme Fatale Dan gives me that sultry little look again and so does Android Dan and I just make up an excuse and lock myself up in the bathroom for a while.

"This," Invincible Alien Dan says, as we float across the featureless vastness that encases Anti-Dan's Universe, "is the Outer Rim. In the six months since Anti-Dan set it up around his Universe, it has hardened to the point where not even my blows or Annihilator Dan's magna-beams can tear through it. We have put up our own defenses in the event that he attempts to break through the siege but . . ."

While Invincible Alien Dan is going on about quantum crossroads and entropic shells, I reach my hand out and run my finger across the Outer Rim's smooth surface. A tiny crack sprouts across the gray face and begins to blossom outward in a spider web pattern, too discreet to make out.

"What's that?" I say, pointing at the widening crack spreading across the rim, if only to keep Invincible Alien Dan from dragging on.

I've barely traced its ragged outline with my bare hands before it starts to get wider. In the blink of an eye, the crack collapses into a hole that grows exponentially across the outer rim of the Anti-Dan's Universe.

"Breach!" Invincible Alien Dan shouts across all channels and the Dan Fleet revs up its engines, ready to storm the breach. Before I know it, I'm in the Cruiser Danatos, with Space Ace Dan blathering on about the breach, zipping across the face of a vast blackness. Under my feet, an engine that burns with blue-hot power purrs as it outruns light itself.

"There it is! Anti-Earth! Anti-Dan's citadel should be ..." Space Ace Dan says as soon as the little orb of blue and green starts to come into view. We're tearing across the atmosphere, watching the planet roll by beneath us. Only then do I notice the gaping metal firepit across the face of the world.

"Where's Australia?" I mutter. Space Ace Dan just laughs.

"Anti-Dan had it repurposed, soon as he broke up with Anti-Mandy. Maybe it got to be too much." Space Ace Dan says.

"Do we all fail? With our Mandys, I mean."

"I wouldn't know, man. I married mine," Space Ace Dan says and he holds up his right hand to show off the cobalt blue hologram on his finger. I'm halfway through reading the rolling digital inscription on its face when a beam of burning light from Anti-Dan's Australian death-cannon tears the Cruiser Danatos clean down the middle and I'm suddenly careening across the air, with nothing but an emergency jetpack to keep me level.

Forty seconds later, I'm skidding across the surface of the Pacific Ocean, heading for where Sydney used to be. From below, a swarm of Anti-Dan robot harriers burst from the ocean floor, talons clicking, off to meet the invading horde of Dans.

"Let's get this ..." I start to say and get a mouthful of water so I settle for keeping my mouth shut. I'm just starting to get bored, when the shoreline of Sydney explodes into a black, *skittering* cloud of inhuman monstrosities that charges at me from every direction.

"Well, that was easy," I say as I look back at the hordes of dismantled Dan-bots, the legion of half-xeno Dan slaves and the crushed champions of the Anti-Dan Universe that have been splayed out in my trail.

"They were the tramplers of Universes. My Anti-matter Horde," Anti-Dan says from atop his throne of Dan skulls and snaking wires. "You took them down in less than fifteen minutes."

"I don't wanna have to brag . . ." I say, blushing. The Anti-Dan rises from his throne, shedding his cloak as he comes down the steps. With a flick of his wrist, a blade of crackling red energy comes to life.

"You can't stop me. I've come too far, sacrificed too much," Anti-Dan says. With a gesture, fractal shards of metal blossom across his body, turning into a writhing suit of armor. An arsenal of impossible weapons sprouts from his back, suspended in the air around him like a deadly mandala.

"Look dude, all you gotta do is stop before you kill everybody. Just . . . tear down this thing, pull back the Null cloud and I swear I'm going back."

"Do you know what they took from me? Those self-serving bastards, do you know what they did to me? To us?" the Anti-Dan cackles and slashes at me again, a half-dozen blows that flash across the air and cut swathes across the ground around me. I roll and I duck and I flail around and somehow come out unscathed, even as his energy blade cuts through concrete and steel frames as if they were made from butter, even as it set fire to the air around us with every swipe.

"They ruined my job!" Anti-Dan howls, as we're rolling across a mountain range, crashing like giants. He slams me through half a mile of granite and I chuck hunks of pyrite at him, torn with my bare hands. Our blows echo like thunder.

"They destroyed my house!" Anti-Dan screams at me, while we're grappling over a pool of molten magma. Below us, the Earth's tectonic plates shiver and slam together, the force of the blow throwing us apart.

We're teetering on the edge of the Australian generator, the Hordes of Dans clashing above us like gods on Judgement Day, when Anti-Dan finally tears his shattered armor off himself and howls:

"They took my Mandy!"

When he lunges at me again, I take a step back and let the momentum carry him past me. He's over the edge before he can react, his red saber tumbling down into the seething darkness and all that's keeping him from falling down into whatever nightmare machine is down there is my own sweaty grip.

"They screwed us over good, didn't they?" I tell him and the horror begins to slip away from Anti-Dan's eyes, replaced by a strange understanding. In that moment, the world-killer facade falls away and I can see, behind all the cosmic villainy and the terror and the Universe-devouring hubbub that he's about as confused and mad about it all as I am so I just help him see the obvious.

"You know, I've got them all here. Every last Dan. You don't even need to fire the damn Null Cloud."

The Anti-Dan stares at me, dumbfounded. Slowly, the realization starts to sink in. When it finally hits home, he grins an all-too-familiar grin.

We settled for a compromise, in the end; Anti-Dan didn't like how I kept him from killing everybody, but trapping every last Dan into a bleak universe that was mostly turned into a weapon of mass destruction wasn't such a bad measure, all things considered.

"They're not gonna starve in there or anything, are they?" I asked.

"Not as long as they don't tear down the automated takeaway joints," the Anti-Dan said, as the Outer Rim healed itself shut behind us.

"That'll do," I said with a shrug.

From the kitchen, Invisible Dan is struggling with his new mitts, working the cast iron skillet over the open fire. It's stir Friday, so dinner's the usual mess of veggies with a sliver of meat and some re-heated Wednesday leftovers, just in case. From the basement, NEET Dan is arguing over the internet with someone from the other side of the world. His online venture hasn't paid out the big bucks yet, but he's chipping in.

"How was work?" Anti-Dan asks, a swarm of reality-bending nanobots sealing up the dimensional tear in the living room.

"You mean flipping burgers and handling fryers for minimum wage in a fantasy land?" I say, and Anti-Dan gives me his signature knowing grin.

"We can always try someplace else. There's gotta be a world where we're up to our eyeballs in cash," Anti-Dan offers.

"Yeah, but it might not have a pair of identical half-elf Mandy twins," I say. Invisible Dan guffaws from the kitchen just before the skillet clatters down onto the floor, making a hot mess all over the linoleum.

"Good one, Dan!" Invisible Dan says. Anti-Dan just shrugs and goes back to shutting down the secret pathways of the Multiverse, one world at a time.

"I'm thinking Dwarf. Who's up for Dwarf?" I say, reaching out for the takeaway menu. Anti-Dan just shrugs. Invisible Dan sticks his mitt out in a thumbs-up. Somewhere outside, there's the distant screech of a manticore-shuttle, flying across the face of an unfamiliar sun.

Konstantine Paradias is a writer by choice. He's published over 100 stories in English, Japanese, Romanian, German, Dutch, and Portuguese and has worked in a freelancing capacity for videogames, screenplays and anthologies. People tell him he's got a writing problem but he can, like, quit whenever he wants, man. His work has been nominated for a Pushcart Prize.

THE POWER OF HATE

By Hugh McStay

Being killed is not at all like is in the movies. There's very little of the dignity afforded to the average person as there is to your standard movie hero. The look of calm resignation that flits across the dying cowboy's face, his eyes gazing off into the eternal distance as his posse stand solemnly by his side, is largely absent for us.

At least in my experience, anyway.

No, the final seconds of my life in this world were not filled with peace and quiet reflection. I thrashed and kicked like a toddler sent to bed early; I fought the inevitable with everything I had. I screamed until my throat felt as though it were being torn apart by fury and desperation. I cried and I wailed as rage burned across my face like a powerful fever. The betrayal coalescing inside me like a fist, beating from my heart and threatening to crack through my chest.

"You have to go mate," he had said, forcing me into the crate at gunpoint.

"You lousy bastard, after everything I did for you!" I shouted.

"Mate, it's over. Just give it up," said Scott. "Like your wife did"

"She knows you're doing this?" I asked.

"Don't be stupid mate. Need to keep her sweet if I'm going to get your business as well. Well, until she has a wee accident like you somewhere down the road."

Scott. The man who took my business, my love, and finally, my life.

I had hired him two months ago. He was an experienced and ruthless salesman who would come to be a huge asset to my dealership. He came with amazing references and I needed someone who could help push the numbers. I had been selling used cars for almost twenty years, my own dealership for the last seven. I was the king of my own little castle, not exactly King Arthur but certainly the hero of my own life. Scott was tall, handsome and clever. He was the kind of guy who was always the centre of any social gathering, who was always full of what my wife called 'banter.' Any women who came to the dealership swooned around him, pestering their husbands to buy the slightly newer model Scott was pushing.

As it turned out, my own wife was also after a new model. I loved that woman with everything I was, from the soles of my feet to my balding patch of grey. Things had been tough for a while; I knew she was unhappy with how the last few years had gone. I was never home and I worked hard to make sure she would never want for anything. But it turned out that I ended up depriving her of the one thing she needed, which was affection and company.

But fucking the younger model and throwing me on the scrap heap? (Well in this case the local lake not half a mile from my home, but you take my point.)

He had ambushed me in the car park as I was packing away my suit jacket into the boot of my car. He struck me across the back of the head with something blunt and metal and the world raced away from me like Usain Bolt on the starting pistol. I awoke by the lake, stripped to my underwear and bound at the wrists. A large wooden crate, big enough for a body, stood ominously beside me.

"In," he insisted.

I charged at him, screaming obscenities I'd be too embarrassed to repeat in polite company. But he had the benefit of both not having his hands bound and not being an out of shape, weak forty-eight-year-old man. He caught me square in the face with the butt of the gun as I reached him, and blackness overtook me once more. When I awoke, I had already been boxed up like a redundant appliance to be sent back to the manufacturer (which was a fairly accurate representation of the facts). I was aware that the box was moving, that Scott was slowly pushing me towards the river.

"Seriously mate, don't worry about a thing. I'll make sure Sarah is well looked after."

The hate bubbled and boiled inside me. I pushed against my confinement but could feel no give in the crate. Scott had been generous with the nails. I felt momentarily weightless as the crate was pushed from the little fishing pier before crashing hard into the water. I began to sink quickly, the freezing water agony against my skin as it rushed in on every side. I kicked and thrashed as hard as I could as the water frothed and splashed. I struggled for my freedom knowing that it would never come.

The thought of Sarah and Scott together was all I could see in the cold dark. My stupidity and naivety for not seeing what was happening before it was much too late. Of him touching her where only I was meant to touch her. Of her enjoying him inside her. Of them laughing at me behind my back, making a fool of me and the life we had led.

My lungs burned as they held on to my final breath. A massive pressure escaped my body as I finally had to give in. The water rushed into my lungs filling them quicker than it had filled the crate. I began to fade from existence, to recede into myself rather than out. I had always imagined my soul floating away from my body like smoke rising from a pyre, but this was not like that at all. As my insides soaked, it felt as though my soul had dried up and shrunk into my chest. The thick lump of hate and rage that had gathered in my final moments became my new form. I inhabited it, hid in it.

And I would grow strong.

The hours became days became weeks. I sat inside my rage, the memories of my human life fading into irrelevancy. I could feel the shell of what I used to be bloating with the water, putrescent and fat. But I did not wither, I did not decay. I grew strong and patient, I focussed on my hate and my anger and it held me together like cement holds together a wall.

Weeks became months.

At last, In the rotting dark, the chest cavity of my former self split open. I rolled out into the crate, the water no longer feeling cold on my form but refreshing. As I pushed myself forward and swam into the dark, a small golden ring passed into my globulous form. Making my way to the cracks in the crate, I pushed my way through, my new body squishing through the slats in the crate like grease down a drain. My world suddenly expanded infinitely. I'd always been told that the soul leaving the body was a beautiful, ethereal thing. But I doubt there was any beauty or divinity at hand that night. I had no eyes as such, but my sight was better than it ever had been, my vision stretching across every centimetre of myself. A gentle current helped move me across the river, pulling me towards one of the large drains at the far side of the lake.

I poured through the thick wire fence and at last came to a stop in a damp pile of waste and garbage. While I could see, my sense of smell and taste had thankfully abandoned me. I flopped forward to escape the worst of the filth only to find that it was trailing with me. I became aware of my new form for the first time out in the open: gelatinous, bilious and very, very green. I looked like the coughed-up phlegm of a giant. I was the embodiment of my hate and anger; my pain and fury held me together like super glue holding together a shattered vase.

The grate led to the dank, rat-infested sewers beneath my sleepy hometown. As I squelched through the mire, the rats fled from me as though I were a threat to them. But my form struggled for firm touch and purchase. I tried repeatedly to grab the various flotsam and jetsam on either side of me, only to watch it all pass through me like a spoon through jelly. I inched through the mire, my hate fuelling my every movement.

That fucking bitch, I thought. *I can't believe I was so blind, I can't believe after all we shared together after all we'd . . .*

I grew bigger with each spiteful thought. Not in my own internal mass, but the filth and grime around me began to attach itself to my form. Through the power of my will, the faeces and discarded waste of my former species formed a crude, perfunctory body. I stumbled as I stood, balance came to me as easily as first steps do. My slime-congealed form stood erect, every inch of my new body felt more a part of me than my own ever had.

And yet, I could already feel it fading. I knew that my time was finite and my power was already leaving me. Whatever dark god had granted me this opportunity would take his payment soon, and I would willingly pay the ferryman when that time came. But not before I had arranged transport for my betrayers.

I hurried my new feet along, sloshing through the dark river beneath me. At last I came to some stairs leading up to street level. I emerged into the night a foul creature of germ and bacteria, of nightmares and impossibilities. And mostly of shit.

I thanked my luck that the lazy bastard couldn't be bothered to get rid of my body further from home, I saw that I was no more than five minutes of stumbling through the Winter night to my destination. I passed by my local shop, the butcher who I used to buy from every weekend, the café that Sarah and I went to every Sunday morning. Sadness began to creep in, infecting my rage with its soft edges. The rudimentary shape that I had assumed began to tremble; I feared that I was going to break down before I achieved my goal. At the thought of it, clumps of my body began to drop from me and splat on the pavement.

No! I thought.

No.

It was the hate that had preserved what I was. It was the need for revenge that had given me form. I screamed into the night sky, the noise that came from what passed as a mouth was like a painful gurgle. My body strengthened, solidified. My renewed sense of purpose hardened both my resolve and my form. I carried on, the cul-de-sac I'd called home for ten years came into view. I marched towards the large house at the end of the street, my beautiful house with its large cherry red door.

"Cherry like your lips," I had once commented to Sarah.

I pushed the door open as softly as my matted paw would allow and passed into my hallway towards the stairs. My choice of cream carpets in the hall had always been folly, never more so than now. I reached the top of the stairs, steaming and furious. I could hear them in my bedroom, grunting and rutting like animals. Sarah, my wonderful Sarah, moaning like a porn star in my bed. Pushing my bedroom door open, I stepped inside to survey the scene.

Scott's arse was thrusting away, both of them enjoying each other, revelling and thriving in my demise. Stepping into the room, Scott was the first to turn.

"What the hell is that smell?" I heard him ask.

Sorry to spoil the mood, I thought as he turned to face me.

If I could have smiled, I would have. The look on his face was worth the trudge alone. He screamed loudly, terrifying Sarah who was still bent over the bed on all fours like an animal. I could see her peering past him at me, then her screams joined his. I doubt many of us expect to be confronted by a shit and bile monster, especially one whose wife you had been fucking.

"What the hell are you?" he asked, his member flopping impotently in my direction.

Advancing on him, Sarah's screams loudened. If I had ears I think they would have been ringing. Scott took a swing at me; his powerful frame threw everything he had into the punch. Connecting with my chest with a wet thump, his fist became lodged squarely where my heart would have been. I stood my ground and watched him stare along the length of his arm in befuddlement. Pulling his shit-encrusted hand from my chest, Scott turned to run to the bathroom. I admired the irony of trying to hide from a shit monster in the bathroom. In his haste, he caught his foot on his hastily discarded jeans and fell hard, face first on the floor.

Still Sarah screamed.

I looked at her, my beautiful wife. She was just as lovely as she was the day we met. I spent the best twenty years of my life with that amazing woman. I loved her with everything that I was.

Tears streamed down her pretty face.

My body began to waver. Whatever black magic responsible for my stay of execution was beginning to slip. My hands broke apart and fell by the wayside. My legs began to tremble. Looking at Scott lying dazed and naked on the floor beside me, I decided that I had one course of action left to me. I fell on him, my coarse disgusting body splattering across his muscular back like a dropped lasagne. The splat seemed to shake him from his daze, his screaming in terror and disgust returned tenfold. I imagine I might have had the same response if someone had dropped 150lbs of faecal matter on me. But it wasn't enough. I had been humiliated, and so now had he.

It wasn't enough.

I pushed.

I felt myself coalesce.

I found my way in.

I slid inside Scott. I funnelled into him like an enema that would never end. Sarah's screams disappeared and all I could hear was the sweet sound of Scott's agony. I poured into him, pushing farther into the soft warmth of his insides. His pain, his unknowable anguish thrilled me, solidified me as I worked my way through him. In the dark, I could hear his flesh tear, his organs rip apart as I pushed farther up his torso. I moved towards the sound from above, his exquisite screaming acting as a beacon in the black. The screaming stopped when I reached his throat, the last of his miserable life pouring out of him as easily as I poured into him.

I pressed on, knowing that our end was near. I pushed into his mouth from his throat, leaving behind my living-waste body which now impaled the length of him. My green, blob-like form was all that remained, and I pressed myself through his open lips, frozen in an eternal, silent scream.

I sit there now, peering out of Scott's mouth. He is stiff and dead on his knees, head cocked back and looking at the ceiling. My ceiling. The thick green creature of hate that grew strong in my corpse is beginning to fade, the dark arts that held me together are losing their hold.

I can see Sarah. She is in the bed still, our bed, staring at her lover's stiff and frozen corpse. With the last of my will, I let go of my centre. I begin to fall apart, my rage spent and gone. Grief overwhelms me as I look at my Sarah, my beautiful Sarah, crying alone in the dark. I break apart and dribble down Scott's chin, like the aftermath of some lewd act. My wedding ring drops from Scott's chin, rolls along the floor to the edge of the bed.

"James?" she whispers as the dark takes me.

"I'm sorry."

Hugh McStay is a native of Glasgow, Scotland, where his love for all things horror blossomed in the city's plethora of urban myths and stories. Influenced by the works of Stephen King and Clive Barker, Hugh has been writing short horror fiction in his spare time for a number of years.

Although a journalism graduate, Hugh has spent the last thirteen years in the customer service industry as a restaurant manager. The sights and sounds of a busy city centre restaurant have shown him the many faces of humanity over the years, from the sublime to the preposterous.

A doting Dad of two beautiful girls, Hugh is a firm believer that his two children are far more formidable than any monster his imagination could ever conjure. Currently working on his first novel, Hugh continues to write short horror stories to delight, disgust and scare in equal measure.

SPIDERING DOWN AN ALLEY

By Jeff Johnson

The six antique electric chairs were arranged in a circle around an alloy pedestal, pointed inward, with people strapped in. Water laid his right hand over the fingernail rakes in the arm of his 1924 Huntsville Edison and felt the needle spike his wrist. There was the almost instant taste of sulfur, and a curling wave of cold railed up the bones of his arm and rinsed his skeleton. He turned to the new guy in chair five and smiled, an expression that had left his face unmapped by lines.

"Frostaay."

The floodlights dimmed and a ghostly, rotating holograph fanned out above the pedestal. News footage out of Hong Kong, less than ten hours old. The CEO of Unitevex had died in the middle of his trial.

Sanchez walked out of the darkness. Suki trailed

behind him, pushing the psychotransmogrification carriage. She took something small from the top instrument tray and laid it in the new guy's lap. Water's eyes narrowed. It looked like a first generation Epsin acoustic modem with rows of Sony zip drives soldered on, all wrapped up in trash wire.

"Joseph C. Beeker winked out from massive heart failure," Sanchez began. "Unfortunately, he departed before the special prosecutor's office could find out what he did with close to nine-hundred-and-sixty million in pension funds. We spidered a roachcam down his alley seventeen minutes and eleven seconds after death and made a firm connection. The roachcam spun back his entrance, and it was—" He clicked the remote in his hand and the spectral hologram blurred. "The interior of an office building."

Water and the other men in the electric chairs shifted in surprise. Sanchez smiled grimly and clicked the roachcam playback into fast forward. It skittered along a gray, windowless wall around a corner into the enormous void of a coliseum, empty of everything except for a desk in the center, where CEO Beeker sat working at a computer.

Water glanced over at Krilanovick, his second-in-command. Krilanovick studied the roach image without expression, but there was a tell in his calm. Suki had put Krilanovick's transmog under his tongue, a shard from a school bus headlamp with an epic tragedy in its past that mirrored some secret in Kril's own history. Krilanovick was carefully rolling the glass back and forth with his tongue.

"This is your drop site," Sanchez continued. "We don't have any data on what to expect in the way of resistance, but my feeling is that CEO Beeker will be the most dangerous variable in this equation." He clicked the roach feed off. "This fucker was so wicked and wrong that he merited an administrative position in Hell, people. Stay sharp. Find that money. This one is going stale fast, so keep an eye on the clock. You have fifteen minutes down there. Make 'em count."

Suki took Water's transmog from the carriage and dropped it in his lap. It was a solid cast iron toy gun with no moving parts, not even a hole in the barrel. The entire thing had been carved and sculpted after being stamped out of old railroad spikes so that it resembled a serpent twisted and tied into the shape of a sixteenth century English Snaphaunce pistol. Water hated the thing almost as much as he hated Suki, the creepy bitch who personally killed all the teams latticing up instead of down. Water had never been up the ladder for Heaven work. He'd heard stories about how Suki liked her job too much when she put the boys going up to Clowntown down for short-term dirt naps.

The countdown began, a luminous green five-sided holograph sprayed from a recessed beak in the pedestal. Twenty seconds. Nineteen. Eighteen.

Suki's cold little hands moved swiftly as she finished her rounds. She used a pink band aid to fix a mummified parrot wing to Pamelar's thin shoulder blade and then briefly massaged Nixon's face before settling a moist white cowl over it. Nixon was a big man, with a quiet voice and not much to say anyway. Water had never really been able to trust him, not completely, because Nixon's transmog was his own face. He turned back to the new guy in chair five.

"That a modem?"

The new guy nodded and forced a smile. He was running pale, with sweat beading on his upper lip. Short, top floor office bulge around the mid-section, small hands and girly wrists. "Yeah. They wrapped it in wire

175

from a Sri Lankan interrogation chamber."

"Won't be any use if there's a fight. Keep to the back until we get to the computer. Don't look at Nixon's face." Water put the bit in his mouth and tightened the chinstrap on his crown.

"I'm just tech support." The new guy sounded breathless.

The clock was down to ten seconds. Water watched as Suki put the bit in the new guy's mouth and wrenched his electrocution crown snugly into place. He turned his eyes back to the clock, almost tasting the green numerals glowing over the steel pedestal. At seven seconds, the Jupiter coil under his chair spun up, tracing the dead man's alley into the afterlife. He thought it sounded like a blend of wind pouring through the bare branches of a dark tree and his grandmother's life of weeping.

At five seconds, Suki backed away into the darkness and the pentagram under the antique electric chairs flared into visibility. The air flooded with ozone and long string polymers. Water held his hand over the big red dead man's button. He was shaking.

The clock hit three and time slowed. He felt a sharp pull at his belly button as the spider tether formed, spooling out Jupiter coils of his lifeline. It always amazed him how much went through his mind in the last few seconds, how long it all seemed. The tech staff told him it was bleed over, a time phase differential from the Jupiter coil establishing itself on his internal chronometer in a three second prelude to eternity.

The ghostly green numeral two formed and Water flicked his eyes to the number five chair, lit from beneath by the numinous glow of the floor's pentagram. The tendons in the new guy's neck stood out like ropes in a rigging, his eyes as wide as eggs in a Cornucopian skull. His white hand was quivering wildly over the new red button on his old Texas Penitentiary smokey. He was all go. Water wondered how they had ruined the little man in the last few hours. Psychotransmogrification had been a hard process when Water had gone through it. It had taken the witchdoctors weeks to find some kind of Pavlov device he could spider in with him, and the resultant holistic descriptor itself always betrayed something profoundly personal about the carrier. He wondered how they had twisted number five's mind to fit him with a modem, the very thing they needed. In Water's case, it was the gun snake in his lap. The others apparently had more imagination, with the possible exception of Nixon.

Water looked back at the clock. One. He sucked at the spit from around his bit and swallowed, then clamped down hard and swallowed again. When the clock hit zero he slammed his hand down on the red button in unison with the others as hard as he could. The currant arced through his freezing bones and his heart stopped mid-beat.

Five dead men spidered down the alley.

Stomachs vomit through the mouth, hearts through the belly button. Water could feel his spider tether in place, a silky braid of terror and raw, jagged insanity, suckling his abdomen like the hickey making party mouth of an ancient, blind fish. He opened his eyes on Beeker's afterlife and screamed.

They were in a high rise of some kind, standing before a window with a panoramic view of a part of hell Water had never seen before. Stretching out below them to the distant, dirty brass horizon was a forest of enormous, Crisco pale tubeworms with glossy black helmets.

In a wandering cilia dance, they seemed to be passing small pink objects between them. Sinuous canyons of what appeared to be molten copper wound through their roots from the west.

Water reeled with vertigo and fell back from the window. The others backed away as he did and professionally cut their own screams, except for the new guy, who had been so paralyzed with terror that he had not made a sound. He tore his eyes from the window and directed at Water an expression made unreadable by its sheer intensity, and then in a spasm clutched his still chest, having just noticed on top of everything else that his heart did not beat in that place.

"We get to sleep in hospital beds tonight," Nixon said softly, trying to calm him.

Krilanovick clapped the new guy on the back. "Maybe Suki'll give you a hand job." Krilanovick had a lisp now that his tongue had merged with his transmog shard of headlamp glass.

"Let's move," Water ordered. "Nixon, you're on point. Pamalar, bring up the rear. New guy stays behind me. Krilanovick, you watch him and guard that modem." He took one last look out the window as Nixon surveyed the blank, gray hallway from the roach playback through the eyeholes in his cowl and then set off to the left, his size sixteen boots just clicks on the stone floor to mark his rolling, bowlegged gait.

They marched in single file, quietly following Nixon. The perfectly square hallway was just what they expected based on the roach feed. CEO Beeker had arrived only a short walk from his eternal post. The view on his arrival was no doubt a message of some sort, tailored to his mind alone.

The gray corridor opened on the chamber from the feed, a massive room empty of everything except a desk in the center where a man sat hunched over a keyboard with his back to them. He raised his head as they approached and turned. Water recognized his profile from the CNN stream.

"So soon," CEO Beeker said calmly as they walked up. He was a smallish man, in a gray suit that matched his surroundings. The suit was one size too large and made him seem paradoxically older and younger, part old man and part baby vulture. He smiled, revealing a distillation of wickedness that took decades to cultivate. His teeth were horse-like and a dull yellow, etched with black fractals. His small, close-set eyes were rimmed with scarlet and the whites were a flat layer of jaundice, mucousy glass and blood film. "I've spent some time self-complicating here, gentlemen. Digging. Eroding. Burping. Unfarming. Your umbilicals . . . You don't belong here." He smiled again.

"Just visiting," Water said. Nixon and Pamalar flanked him, eyes scanning every direction. Krilanovick guided the trembling tech to Beeker's computer and tossed a thumb at it, motioning him to get in and do the deal. The new guy didn't make a move. He stared at the computer and clutched the nest of Sri Lankan interrogation wires to his chest.

"Pensions," Water said evenly. "You tell us where they are, maybe you get a second chance."

"How?" CEO Beeker asked, cocking his head. He pushed away from his desk and casually crossed his legs.

"We're here," Water said. "We're not permanently dead. We can spider you out on one of our tethers. It won't be your body you go back to. That's gone. You might wind up in a monkey or a cat. They don't tell me what they have in the lab. If you're lucky it will be some brain-dead bum or a blank dumpster baby and you can go for full integration."

"You said maybe," Beeker repeated with a fractal flicker of humor. "And my choices range from animals to blind syphilitics of indiscriminate age."

Water narrowed his eyes and brought out one of his best lines, the one he considered the closer.

"I hate this job, Beeker. No, really. I don't like killing myself, however temporary it may be, just so I can rip on down to Hell to haggle with a total piece of shit like you. And they always haggle. Every time. But I write the reports, so spit up now and take whatever body they have for you, but do it fast, or I'll report that you were a Hell-wrecked nut job with no possible retrieval. And I can report whatever I want, because they aren't going to come down here and check."

"Maybe he want to stay," Krilanovick lisped, playing his part. "'Thilly Coo Coo bird."

"What assurances do I have that you can get me out?" Beeker asked. The guy had balls.

"None," Water replied. In fact, there was no way they could bring CEO Beeker back. There never had been. Generally, these interviews went differently in that the subject grasped at any possible hope, no matter how remote.

Beeker shrugged. "You can't take it with you. Bearer bonds. Look for them in the southeast corner of my Aspen retreat. Big safe in a shallow grave." He held his hands out, wrists up in submission.

"Krilanovick," Water ordered.

Krilanovick bumped the frozen tech guy, who staggered to Beeker's computer and stared at it, then connected the modem into the back with some kind of transmog worm with a tiny beak tip. Water watched as the ash-colored monitor pulsed and the Sony micro vaults spiking from dial modems blinked green with access. Beeker stood and backed away from the desk under

Nixon's cowled scrutiny. The tech sat down, hacked the keyboard for less than twenty rapid strokes and then turned to Water.

"Big download," he announced tonelessly. "I don't think we can even get a fraction of it. I've never seen anything like . . ." He trailed off. "Maybe five minutes until the micro vaults are loaded."

"You shouldn't have touched that," Beeker said, sing song. He raised his hands and slowly backed away. "They won't like that."

Water pointed the gun snake at Beeker's forehead.

"And you won't like spending eternity with the IQ of a mushroom. Don't fucking move. Heads up, boys. We're about to have company."

The gun torsioned in Water's grip like a dynamo. A mouth flared at the iron tip of the barrel. Spirals of crimson and wasp abdomen patterns rippled along the surface. Behind him he could hear the shard of headlamp glass clicking between Krilanovick's molars. Pamelar had dropped his shirt to the ground and stood with his naked torso exposed, looking down the corridor behind them. Nixon was still, staring at CEO Beeker through his eyeholes.

Water kept the gun trained on Beeker as he swiveled his head. Pamelar walked a dozen steps away and his wing flicked out, leaving a trail of smoke behind as he flexed. Match light fire flickered along the length of the sinewy thing. He curled it into a tight 'S' around his body and waited, a smoke-shrouded form lit in guttering light. Krilanovick backed up against Water and tested his tongue. It flicked out nearly fifty feet in a chameleon's flycatcher snap. The barb of the now diamond hard glass left a long, scorching furrow on the concrete floor. Nixon just stared at CEO Beeker, utterly motionless.

"Mother of—," the new guy began.

"Don't," Water snapped. "It draws them like fruit flies."

There was a tense silence, broken only by the load profile beep on the micro vaults and the chitinous pops from Pamelar's wing spiral. The massive room had five entrances, including the one they had come through. They lacked the ornamentation Hell was famous for, and everything was International Style instead, which was a fresh form of awful.

Five little girl dolls in matching orange prison coveralls stepped out of one of the square corridor entrances, carbon copy smiles on their identical sooty faces.

"Daddy!" they chirped in unison. One of Water's men just had dead mare, a very personal kind of bummer.

"End 'em all!" Water roared. The snake gun transmog had the longest range, so he drew a bead on the middle doll and fired. The muzzle of the gun flared like a rectum and spat a tooth that traveled the distance in less than a second. It hit the little girl in the center square in the forehead and she exploded into a pile of spiders. The darkness in the corridor behind her roiled like a mud pit full of eels and Nixon moaned softly as his face charged. Water fired a wrist pounding machinegun, bursting into the black cavity, and then wheeled to vomit some fire down the next opening. The gun snake was hot and the rounds came out as complete dentures that left foamy contrails of asparagus green.

"Everyone behind Nixon!" Water screamed.

CEO Beeker began cackling wildly. Pamelar wreathed himself in a flaming parrot wing and turned to Water, closed his eyes. The new guy looked at the computer and then at Water, beyond scared once again. Krilanovick caught it and tackled him. Nixon stepped in front of Water, facing outward as the main assault began.

As the big man raised his cowl, Water realized why Beeker was crowing with delight.

The dolls were nothing but spiders when the boiling thing came out of the dark behind them. It was more than ten feet tall, with stork legs thinner than the new guy's wrists, moist as newborn bird necks and festooned with random and multiple knees. On top was a head shaped like the body of a guitar, big side up, with two rolling eyes. The jaw hung down a good three feet and clamped in its wobbling mouth was an antique mirror. The head swiveled right at Nixon as he raised his cowl. Water closed his eyes and fired blindly as the screaming started all around him. There was an explosion as he hit something and he knew, he knew he had to look, but he had seen what happened when anything looked upon Nixon's transmog face, and it took more effort than electrocuting himself over a Jupiter coil in a Texas pen mercy seat to do it.

The first thing he saw was Pamelar, frozen for all of eternity in a hell within Hell itself. His body was concrete, already gathering dust, and the look of horror on his screaming face, fixed at the peak of a spasm of something so wrong he no longer resembled a sentient being, broke something in Water. He lowered his gun and surveyed the ruin.

The mirror walker was down, seizing violently. Beeker was still crooning, doing a jig with his eyes closed, capering in a loose circle. Nixon was frozen too, his transmog forever pointed at itself in some way, but his back was to them and whatever was broken in Water knitted itself in some small way when he knew he wouldn't have to see what had happened above Nixon's neck. The stony fingers jutting from the back of the man's head were bad enough.

"Water," Krilanovick wept. "Water, Water, Water,

Lt., shoot that song off."

Water raised his transmog and shot CEO Beeker through the Adam's apple. His musical interpretation of his inner world only went dead for everything outside of his head, because he kept right on dancing.

"Open your eyes," Water ordered. "Krilanovick. Open up. Get New Guy and his wire box. Point at the sound of my voice and open your eyes."

Krilanovick shuddered and raised his head. The new guy, the geek, was prostrate underneath him and didn't move. Since no one was breathing, it was hard to tell if he was dead dead, but Water didn't think so. Krilanovick's eyes went from Water to Nixon's frozen back and then to Pamelar. His face twisted with rage and he turned his glare on CEO Beeker, who was still doing his touchdown spaz.

"We. Are. Leaving," Water said quietly. Some kind of pitter patter, the sound of a trillion white mice, was echoing out of one of the corridors. Something was coming. They needed to spool their umbilical tethers in as tight as possible before they sent a signal to have the Jupiter coil reel them back, which meant they had to get as close as they could to where they came in. Krilanovick's eyes flicked back to Water and he stared without recognition.

"C'mon, Kril. Get the new kid," Water whispered. "Get that box."

Krilanovick rose and pulled the technician to his feet, thrust the wire modem into his hands. The guy's slack face was so empty that it was clear that his mind was way, way gone. Water looked back the way they had come. It was clear. He took one more look at CEO Beeker and then shot the computer, pulling the trigger on his transmog hard enough to get the dentures again. The desktop exploded and Beeker froze. His red eyes widened and his smile vanished, replaced by awe as what had happened dawned on him.

Cursed to an eternity of boredom, with nothing but spiders and mice for company, and without a voice to sing to them.

Water ran. Behind him Krilanovick dragged their failing zombie. In a tight cluster, they made their way like that, with Water in the lead, his transmog irised and held at arm's length in front of them, pulsing and rippling, Krilanovick two steps behind pushing the new guy and keeping his own transmog poised. They made it back to the window and both of them looked out one final time as Water hastily prepared to draw the Jupiter beacon. Krilanovick barked something incoherent.

The giant waxen tubeworms with the black helmets, rising from the river of molten copper, were more clearly visible now that the fine smog that had hung around them had cleared. The tiny pink things, thousands upon thousands upon endless thousands of them that they were passing along between them, were naked, screaming people.

Water knelt and traced a pentagram on the floor, moving fast. It glowed with Jupiter light, but it was very faint. The alley was closing. He followed the lines again, quicker now, and the light grew brighter. Again, and again, he wrote it, faster and faster until his arm was an unnatural blur, and just as he heard Krilanovick scream that they weren't alone, he slammed his palm down in the center of the diagram, the same motion he had made when he slammed the suicide button on his Lone Star Sparkey. His belly button burned like a collapsing star and—

Water opened his eyes slowly. The room was white. There was a distant beeping. He licked his lips. He was dry. His eyes were dry. So was his mouth. He didn't know where he was, but he knew he had been very, very sick. He felt light, like all of his muscle and fat had been burned away by fever. He blinked and almost didn't open his eyes again.

"Water. Eugene Water." It was a man's voice, quiet. *Water*, he thought. *I am Water.* He opened his eyes again and lolled his head to the side. Sanchez was sitting next to the bed. He realized he was in a bed. A hospital bed. Sanchez was sitting in a chair. A hospital chair.

"Krilanovick," Water rasped. Sanchez tilted his head sideways, then looked away.

"Second Lieutenant Krilanovick was in a coma for three weeks after we cut him out of his Yellow Edison. His... his crown melted on uptake. He..." Sanchez trailed off.

Water thought about that. Kril had a wife and a kid with some kind of smile. Kril, who liked to BBQ even when it rained, especially when it rained. Kril, who liked to play Frisbee. Kril, Gulf War vet, three times decorated, who had been plucked from more than a hundred thousand soldiers with detailed psyche profiles, just like all forty-seven of them in Project Afterlife, the rare selection of the psychotransmogrification PhD's and the research staff, for reasons no one ever talked about. Kril, who died in the World. Kril, who might not be anywhere, anymore.

"The uh, the new guy?"

Sanchez sighed. "He never really made it back. Name was Riley Koch. His profile read like a pervy horror movie shown upside down in a slaughterhouse, so I can't say I'm too sorry about it. Made Nixon look like a choir-boy from Disneyland fantasy church. He regained consciousness after four days and asked if someone could wheel him outside. Doc on rotation said a few minutes might even be good for his lungs, so they put him in a wheelchair and took him out into the courtyard. Looked at the tree out there for about a minute and died. Just . . . turned off. Autopsy team, well, there were people in from DC, Cedar Sinai, even Germany. Never did figure it out, but his body. It wouldn't burn, so no cremation. Buried at Bethesda, but all the grass died so he was reinterred somewhere in Louisiana."

"Riley Cooch," Water said softly.

"Koch," Sanchez corrected. "As in, eh, Koch."

Water cleared his throat and tried to sit up. He was a good thirty pounds lighter and too weak to do it. He raised his arm and the brittle, wasted thing he saw brought up a wave of sadness, the peculiar variety of heartbreak he'd felt when his childhood cat had been put to sleep. The lost brand of sorry sad.

"How . . . how long . . ."

"Seven weeks," Sanchez said, gently pushing him back. He raised a cup of water to Water's lips and waited while he spluttered through a sip before continuing. "You were in a coma until this morning. The fever was terrible. Thirty-one days of it. The, ah. I'm not going to lie to you, Water. There was some brain damage. We won't know until . . . Tests."

Water didn't say anything for a long time. He wandered around in his mind looking for things, but he didn't know what he was looking for, and that told him enough.

"Suki," he whispered finally. Sanchez nodded and rose to his feet. He looked down at Water for a long time and then, finally, saluted. Water stared at the ceiling and waited, and eventually he heard the door open and close.

Suki appeared in his field of vision. She smiled with her mouth, but her eyes remained insect hard.

"Suki."

"First Lieutenant Water."

Water held his hand out and Suki took it. She sat. Water tilted his head sideways and they stared into each other's eyes.

"The micro vaults," Water said. "The Sony micro vaults. What did, what was on Beeker's computer?"

"Terabytes," Suki answered. "A map. A map like no one has ever imagined. Cartography itself as a science made a huge leap forward. There are things, things no one ever imagined. But we only got a fragment of what was there."

Water didn't say anything.

"There was a lot from CEO Beeker," Suki went on. "About thirty percent of what was captured was what he had been entering. Uncounted pages, but there really wasn't any point in counting them in the end. A computer network is running it for a final count."

"Why?"

"He only wrote five sentences, over and over and over again. We checked for a pattern, some king of hidden relevance, but there wasn't anything. We had every kind of specialist we could think of look at it. They all came away empty."

"What was it?"

Suki cleared her throat and recited from memory. When she spoke, Water could hear in the pauses every period, and in every syllable the cracks between the spaces inside the lines. There was enough Water for that.

"bright, bright
  my new bank will have these children
    who eat—eat

the seeds for eating—eating"

When she was done they sat in silence.

"It was written that way. Over and over. If it were printed, it would be on a paper that would wrap around the world until all the earth was white with it, white with paper and letters too small to read."

Eventually Water spoke, the last words he would ever speak.

"Suki. When you kill for the lattice ride up to Clowntown, why does your soul stay?"

Suki took a syringe from her lab coat pocket and thumbed the cap off, met Water's eyes. He nodded, pleading, and she injected the lethal dose of potassium chloride into his IV.

"Eugene. I don't have a soul. Belief is a terrible, terrible vice. The dirty screen door in Heisenberg, where Plank left his keys for Socrates—"

His eyes closed, and Water was silent.

Jeff Johnson is a full time screenwriter and novelist who divides his time between Portland and Los Angeles. He's the author of the critically acclaimed *Tattoo Machine*, Spiegel & Grau 2007, as well as *Everything Under The Moon*, *Knottspeed, A Love Story*, the *Lucky Supreme series* (Publisher's Weekly Starred Review) *Lucky Supreme, A Novel of Many Crimes*, *A Long Crazy Burn*, and *The Animals After Midnight*, and *Deadbomb Bingo Ray*. His latest short story, "Cantina Kinjiku," will appear in the upcoming *Killer Crimes Anthology*, alongside Stephen King and Joyce Carol Oates. Literary representation is Mark Gottlieb at the Trident Media Group. The *Lucky Supreme series* was recently also acquired by Italian publisher Fanucci.

Current television projects with Tom Hildreth of Sternman Productions include *Lincoln Park*, a police drama set in Portland, Maine, *Millinocket*, a political comedy-drama set in Millinocket, Maine, *Sternman*, a crime drama set on the Maine coast, and *Lune*, a horror-fantasy, based on his acclaimed 2016 novel *Everything Under The Moon*.

LAST OF THE AZTEC RIDERS

By Mark Mellon
(Originally published in *Deadman's Tome*)

"Buy me a beer and I'll tell you a good story."

Jack Pilgrim regarded the one-eyed, one-armed, huge man on the barstool beside his. The half of his face minus an eye was scarred almost beyond recognition as human, his deformed lip pulled down in a perpetual half scowl. After twelve hours on his hog, high on meth, Pilgrim only wanted to focus on the shot and the beer before him, drunk, to delay and lessen the inevitable bummer.

"Look at the patch on my cut."

He turned his back to Pilgrim. On the faded black leather vest, a skull with a feathered headdress screamed. The top rocker read "Aztec Riders," the bottom said "Tiny."

"I'm the only one allowed to wear this patch, man. Nobody left but me. And I can tell you all about it, the whole freaked out story. But you gotta buy me that beer first, man. So, what do you say?"

Intrigued and sympathetic to a biker so fucked up he'd never ride again, Pilgrim nodded to the bartender who poured a draught Bud in a pint glass and set it before Tiny. He knocked it back, set the glass on the bar, and wiped the foam from his scraggly beard with his hand.

"Like I said, I'm the only Aztec Rider left. You should've seen us back in the day, bombing a hundred strong in a tight vee formation at eighty per, total road Nazis, blowing through every traffic light. And no one, not no citizen, not no pig, dared fuck with us. We had Bullhead City under our thumb and most of Nevada and Arizona too, at least as far as pussy and meth went. And it was all because of our Prez, Pothunter. See, we called him Pothunter coz he was always poking around in caves on Federal parks and reserves, looking for Indian stuff, old shit, know what I mean? Even if it is a Federal beef. Like we cared about stuff like that. And then he showed up at the clubhouse with this idol, like a real idol, you know—"

The clubhouse was a long, one story cinderblock building with a corrugated iron roof in the middle of the desert, surrounded by a ten foot fence topped by concertina barb wire with signs posted that read: KEEP OUT! and TRESPASSERS WILL BE SHOT! in huge, screaming red letters. Inside the dimly lit clubhouse, the Riders sheltered from the roasting heat to the dull roar of a sorely overtaxed wall unit air conditioner, ripped off from a hotel. In the background, John Kay rumbled, "*Close*

your eyes, girl, Step inside, girl," on the tape deck while Tiny snorted yet another line of meth. The room became infinitely extended in his tunnel vision. Blood pounded in his ears like hammers against anvils. He wondered if he was going to pass out.

The door burst open. The blast of light and heat sent the Riders scurrying to darkness like rats to their holes. Pothunter walked in, a burlap bag held in both hands. A prospect hurried to shut the door.

"Hey, Prez. What you got? Beer or scotch, I hope," Tiny said.

Pothunter set the dusty bag on the already filthy carpet.

"Lots better, Tiny. I went to Teuwanta State Park and dug some by the cliffs. You won't believe what I found."

He undid the rope and pulled down the bag to reveal a terra cotta figure about two feet high, ancient and worn, the paint faded, the features still distinct. The idol was a hideously grimacing, round-headed skeleton, dressed in a mask and garments made from flayed human skin. Internal organs, liver, heart, and kidneys, dangled from an open chest cavity.

"Whoa. What the fuck is that thing, Prez?" almost everyone said simultaneously.

"Our new mascot."

Pothunter's broad, red face beamed with pleasure. Tiny had never seen him happier, not even when he beat a Red Devil to death with a chain. He picked up the idol and set it with great ceremony on the card table that held the club's shrine, composed of pictures of members who were either dead or in prison and some fake Indian relics Pothunter bought in Nogales one time.

"Listen up, everybody. This is the first real find I ever made. It's some kind of god, some kind of bad, evil thing that just lives to make trouble. You know, like us. This is bringing us wicked good luck. So, I declare a three-day party in honor of our new mascot, the god of the Aztec Riders. Bad Bob, tell the mommas to haul ass over here. They got some trains to pull."

"Bitching," Tiny bellowed.

The others howled as well, more delighted by the prospect of days of sex, booze, and meth than the idea of an official mascot. Head bent, arms pumping, Pothunter shuffled back and forth before the idol in his own version of a ritual dance. Puzzled and somewhat disturbed by the grotesque figure, like the loyal members they were, others showed club spirit and followed the Prez's lead. They danced behind him in strict order of precedence, Vice Prez Bad Bob, Secretary Tiny, Treasurer Vulture Ed, and Sergeant of Arms Bruiser Vito, followed by patch members in order of seniority. Prospects brought up the rear. The Indian Dance became a ritual, a ceremony that set the Riders apart and drew them together.

"Swear to God, if our luck didn't change the day Pothunter found that idol. Like bam, like the biggest, best hit of meth you'd ever want in your life. In no time, we had a steady stable of a dozen whores, each one turning over eighty percent of everything she made in tricks. She'd a fucking well better if she didn't want her ass beat. Plus, we had five meth labs going, no bucket shop shit either, man, each one with a real cook who knew his stuff cold. And no cop ever so much laid a finger on us, not one bust in the whole club for eight months, I shit you not."

Tiny paused to give Pilgrim a significant look with his pale blue orb.

"Storytelling's thirsty work, you know."

Pilgrim nodded again. The bartender set another Bud before Tiny. He knocked it down like the first.

"Yeah, so like I said, we was rolling in serious bread after years of nickel and dime bullshit. We knew we was lucky and Pothunter was right. The idol brought us luck. Every weekend we threw a party with enough booze, drugs, and sluts to do up Vegas, and live bands too. And the big climax was always the Indian Dance in front of the idol. Man, you should have seen how we used to get into it. It was downright tribal, know what I mean?"

Tiny frowned with the good side of his face and shut his eye.

"And everything was cool, man, just completely cool, until this bitch came along one night and really started some shit, you know—"

The sun was a bloody red eye above the horizon. Clean, fine desert air was marred by the stink of tobacco and marijuana smoke, silence shattered by pounding drums and twanging guitars.

"And this bird you cannot change," a three-hundred-pound man in a tiny black cowboy hat wailed from the stage as his band thrashed through primitive chords behind him.

Tiny took a drag off a giant reefer to take the edge off the speed tweaking through his veins and stared at bare breasts flaunted by drunken mommas as they gyrated to the music. He caught Bad Bob's eye and stuck out his tongue. Bad Bob made a fist and pumped it up and down, the universal symbol for a gang bang.

The night wore on. A select few outsiders were allowed inside the clubhouse to party with the Riders, primarily hangers on and attractive women. Flush with cash, the Riders had refurbished the clubhouse, equipped with a new pool table, fully stocked wet bar, and an impressive new shrine, handcrafted from mahogany by a full patch member who also held down a righteous day job as a cabinet maker. The idol was in its own special niche, topped by a banner that depicted the Riders' crowned, screaming skull.

Lines of meth were laid out on a table, straws alongside for anyone who cared to snort. The open bar was staffed by two succulent, young honeys, enormous fake breasts straining against ridiculously tiny t-shirts to the point of rupture. As always, Steppenwolf blared, only now from a state of the art MP4 player.

"Last night I found Aladdin's lamp . . ."

The scene was lively, the vibe as mellow as could be among a gang of violent felons high on hard drugs. Tiny tried to take it all in, perception fractured by alcohol and drugs until moments became difficult to link together. He took another drag off the joint, exhaled, and went into a coughing fit.

A loud, brassy, female voice cut through the party chatter and music like a semi-trailer's klaxon in the desert night.

"So, what the fuck is that supposed to be? Santa Muerte or something?"

A fortyish Latina woman drunkenly swayed in the middle of the room, attractive even though overweight, jet black hair flecked with a few silver threads, a loose grin on her face, eyes wide and full of devilry. Miller tall boy in one hand, she pointed at the idol. Wild, chaotic laughter burst from her.

"Where did you gringos find that? In Tijuana? I bet you paid way too much."

"Listen, bitch, that's our club mascot, so don't disrespect it, you hear me," Pothunter bellowed, his ordinarily red face a brighter shade of beet. "That's a genuine pre-Columbian artifact I dug up myself out at Teuwanta State Park."

"Are you kidding me? Where I come from in Guerrero, factories make stuff like that by the shit ton. *Dios mio, que gringo tontería.*"

"No, bitch, you're wrong. This is the genuine, real thing that I dug up with my own hands. And I'm gonna prove what I mean right now. Members. It's time for the Indian Dance."

Pothunter dropped low and began the familiar wind milling shuffle. The other Riders fell in behind him with the precision of a well-rehearsed dance team. Back and forth they danced before the idol in zigzag lines, each man caught up in the intricate dance steps, faces serious and grave.

"Oh, shit, I can't believe this shit. This has got to be the funniest fucking thing I've ever seen. *Ay, que broma.*"

Her beer gut rhythmically shook with laughter, the whites of her eyes and teeth flashing in the black strobe light.

"Bitch, I've had fucking enough of you," Pothunter screamed.

He ran over to the woman, and with one vicious uppercut, knocked her sprawling, out cold before she even hit the linoleum. Tiny put two fingers to his mouth and blew out a long, loud appreciative whistle.

"Down with one sock. That's why Pothunter's Prez. Yes, sir, Aztec Riders forever."

The Indian Dance continued. The woman lay where she fell, ignored by everyone. The night wore on. Before Tiny knew it, sense of time destroyed by drugs, it was three in the morning and no one in the clubhouse but the few most hardened partiers and the unconscious woman.

"Tiny, chop up some more flake."

"Sure thing, Prez."

Tiny dumped a hefty pile of meth flake onto a mirror and chopped it fine with his buck knife. The woman on the floor moaned loudly. Pothunter looked over at her and grinned.

"Looks like she's coming 'round. Good thing too. Now we can kick her ass out."

She sat up and cradled her aching jaw in her hands.

"Oh, you motherfuckers. You cracked my tooth."

She looked up and focused on Pothunter.

"You're a real brave man, you are, punching a woman. *Que hombre.*"

"Yeah, well, you see what you get, bitch, when you disrespect the Aztec Riders," Pothunter said.

She got to her feet, still good and drunk and plenty angry too.

"Disrespect a bunch of pussy, *pinche* cocksuckers like you, you fucking gringo. I got *chulo* buddies that eat little shits like you alive. Fuck you and fuck your stupid idol most of all. *Pendejo joto cabron.*"

She spat at Pothunter.

"Bitch, I've had just about enough of your fucking shit," Pothunter said.

He ran over to the woman, knocked her flat again, and kicked her repeatedly with his steel toed Chippewa boots. Other Riders joined in, punched and kicked her as she writhed and screamed on the floor.

"Hold her down. Hold the fucking cunt down," Pothunter ordered.

Riders pinned down her arms and legs. Bad Bob crooked a massive arm around her head and pinned her jaws shut. Pothunter took out his Bowie knife with the sixteen-inch blade. He slit the woman's shirt open, bared her soft, unmuscled gut. Tiny's eyes went wide with joy. He loved nothing better than a gangbang.

Pothunter raised the knife high over his head. The woman's eyes went wide with fear. She tried to break free, but half a dozen bikers held her down hard.

"Now you're going to pay for your fucking disrespect, cunt."

"No, Prez, no," Tiny bellowed. "Not in front of witnesses."

Pothunter's knife stabbed down, deep into the woman's stomach, just below the sternum.

The scream that poured through her clenched teeth deafened everyone in the clubhouse, a horrible, mortal wail of pain. Pothunter nonetheless dug the cruel blade in deeper, wrenched her stomach open into a gaping wound.

"We're gonna worship the idol the real way, the Aztec way."

Deep into shock, her eyes rolled back into her head. Her body thrashed uncontrollably. Beer gutted bikers could barely hold her down. Pothunter jammed his right hand into the open wound. He fished around for a moment, grunted with satisfaction when he found what he wanted, and with one, awful, tearing wrench, yanked her heart loose from its main strings.

The screams ended. The woman lay still, quite dead. Covered with gore, Pothunter stood tall and proud. In his bloodstained hand, to the Riders' awe and terror, a still beating heart. Black blood oozed from ventricles.

"This is just like the Aztec priests did it, brothers. Good enough for them, good enough for us. This is going to change our luck forever."

He took the heart and held it high before the idol.

"Accept our sacrifice."

Pothunter smeared the idol with the heart. Blood stained the idol's face. Pothunter smiled widely, drunkenly, well pleased with his handiwork.

There was an awful thunderclap, a crash of doom like the last trump. The lights went out.

"What the fuck happened?"

A grotesque figure appeared before them. A skeletal corpse cladded in another man's flayed hide crouched before them, the idol brought to life. Internal organs dangled from his open chest cavity, lungs, liver, and beating heart. The god's unsmiling mouth protruded slightly from the splayed lips of the expertly-skinned face that covered his own. Vertical stripes ran down the mask. The flayed man's hands hung loose by his wrists. Long tassels hung down his back from his elaborate, green-feathered headdress. Beneath the flayed garments, yellow skin was painted red. Blood and pus seeped to the floor from the abscesses and open sores that covered his body. The smell of rotting flesh was unbearable. Blue flames burned in the flayed mask's eyeholes, the only light in the otherwise black clubhouse.

Pothunter smiled broadly. He pointed to the bizarre apparition and gestured widely to his brothers.

"Do you see this shit? It fucking works. Everybody get down on your knees and bow."

Addled with drugs and adrenaline, caught up in the moment, the Riders automatically did as their Prez bid. They got down on their knees and bowed low to their mascot made flesh. Pothunter even made so bold as to approach the idol and present the heart to the idol, thick blood caked on his hand.

The apparition's face split wide in a soundless roar. So did the flayed skin of the victim's face. The skin ripped into pieces to reveal the wearer's broad-nosed, cat-mouthed face, only to have that split wide as well. With a great gush of blood and splintered bone, the face destroyed itself to show a new one. The tiny, fine-haired head of a squalling infant screamed for his mother's dug only to also split wide with a violent wrench of flesh and bone to show a handsome, young man, red face smooth and unlined. The handsome face seamed down the middle and ripped in twain. There in its place stood the withered, drooling countenance of an incredibly old man, only to have the hoary face crack in turn to show the grinning skull that lurks under every human face.

Bits of bloody flesh and fragments of shattered bone spattered Pothunter's face. Slack-jawed with fear, eyes fixed on the exploding head despite the endless spray of gore, Pothunter managed to scream at last, a long and low, pitiful wail like a small animal about to die.

The idol stuck his long nails like daggers into Pothunter, ripped him to literal shreds before the other Riders like an angry child with a newspaper.

"Shit. Run for it."

Riders ran for the door, but it was padlocked shut and the lock wouldn't turn. A few men had enough nerve to pull their pieces and fire at the monster. Bullets riddled the walking corpse, but it just kept on coming, a trail of gore and lymph behind it. Grim face indifferent to their misery behind his flayed mask, he inflicted the same fate on each man, tore them into bloody gobbets of meat, rent them asunder limb from limb. Brave men who'd sworn never to crumble or bend the knee, each begged for mercy in his turn, called out for his mother, only to be tortured to death, maimed and savaged until he died with a last, despairing cry.

Tiny found himself outside the compound with no idea how he got there. His right arm hung useless and shattered by his side. Blood streamed from the ruins of his left eye socket. In the distance, he could hear a siren's wail, a police car or an ambulance. Tiny stumbled toward the approaching siren, his only hope for survival.

"And that's the straight and narrow of it, swear to God on a stack of Bibles before my mother's grave, every last word of it. Only thing I can't figure out is why I was the only one to get out of it, even if it wasn't in one piece."

"Because you told your Prez to stop before he killed the woman," Pilgrim said.

Tiny considered this, then shrugged.

"Maybe so, but it's still about the Goddamnedest thing I ever saw. Think you wanna stand me another beer, man? Just one bro helping another, you know?"

Pilgrim pulled out his trucker's wallet and put three twenties down on the bar.

"Keep the change," he told the bartender.

He headed toward the door only to have a painfully thin blonde woman intercept him. One even more than passably pretty, her delicate features were ravaged and gaunt from hard living.

"You didn't believe that line of bullshit he was handing out, did you?" she said with a conspiratorial grin, teeth blackened from meth abuse. "He just blew himself up cooking meth, that's all. You ain't headed to Kingman, are you? I'm not too proud to slut a ride, if you know what I mean. You got any meth on you?"

"Sorry. I ride alone."

Pilgrim went through the batwing doors, outside into heat that smothered him like a funeral pall. He saddled his Indian, kick started the engine, and drove off into the night.

Mark Mellon is a novelist who supports his family by working as an attorney. Short fiction by Mark has recently appeared in *Suspense Magazine*, *Yellow Mama*, and *Thuglit*. Four novels and over fifty short stories have been published in the USA, UK, and Ireland. A novella, *Escape From Byzantium*, won the 2010 Independent Publisher Silver Medal for F/SF.

OATS STUDIOS: Volume 1— "Rakka," "Firebase," and, "Zygote"

A Gehenna Post Review

(Originally Published in the Gehenna Post)

PART 1: Rakka

Greetings from the Nether Realm,

Director Neill Blomkamp has proven himself time and again as an innovative director, bringing to life such films as District 9 (2009), Elysium (2013), and Chappie (2015). It was rumored a few years ago that Blomkamp was working on an Alien (1979) film that would continue the franchise directly picking up where James Cameron's Aliens (1986) left off. Such characters as Michael Biehn's Corporal Hicks and Sigourney Weaver's Ellen Ripley were due to reprise their roles. However, after the considerable backlash and critical polarization concerning Elysium and Chappie, it seemed that the Alien project was all but lost in developmental hell.

When OATS Studios was announced, and it was confirmed that Neill Blomkamp would be directing several short horror and science fiction films, many moviegoers and fans alike were thrilled to see what the polarizing director could bring to the table. He did not disappoint.

The first chapter of the first volume for OATS Studios is a short titled, "Rakka," starring, you guessed it, Sigourney

Weaver. It follows humanity's resistance to an alien invasion, where the extra-terrestrial beings experiment and torture humans in ways that are both grotesque and enthralling. Blomkamp's signature direction is at play here, housing many fantastic and nail-biting sequences while also never finding reluctance in showing brutal imagery that can make viewers of a weaker stomach queasy.

The feelings of hopelessness and chaos ensue rather quickly, as we delve deeper into the makings of these monsters. Several events occur that prelude to a sequel in Volume 2, as is the uniform occurrence in each short. The CGI is fantastic in this short film, the aliens never short of seeming authentic and terrifying. "Rakka" brings a whole new level of fear for alien invasion to the screen, making it difficult to imagine how our species could ever survive against such vile and disgusting creatures.

The practical effects that Blomkamp is known for, and his propensity for realistic gore, are both on display here. The visceral nature of the violence compliments the director's previous work, once more emphasizing the director's knack for combining beautiful cinematography with unsettling events onscreen. The plot is interesting enough and definitely keeps the viewers anxious and excited for the next installment.

OUR RATING: 4/5 STARS

PART 2: Firebase

Based during the Vietnam War, this short film revolves around a soldier who is hunting a supernatural being named the River God. We won't dive too deep into what or who the River God is, but between this monster's invulnerability and apparent loss of humanity, there is something deep about the villain of "Firebase" that makes it difficult to take sides. When the creature's origin is finally revealed, it forebodes a sense of karma and justice for the atrocities that were the Vietnam War.

Blomkamp cleverly mashes sickening sequences of grotesque gore with mind-numbing and hallucinogenic moments that will also lend a sensational drug-induced stupor to the viewer. The CGI is once again masterful, never rendering the story unbelievable or flimsy. "Firebase" launches with dread from the opening sequence, and unlike its predecessor and successor, this short is a slow burning match that culminates to yet another cliffhanger, making us beg for more.

The methodically-paced grimness that encompasses "Firebase" is complimentary to the setting and topic of the Vietnam War. Blomkamp utilizes many interesting techniques to make the short feel "vintage" in a way. These moments, coupled with believable characters and dialogue, strike a certain chord with our notions of this dark era in the United States. Despite having a few plot points that are either cliched or lacking of genuine creativity, Blomkamp compensates with illustrious scenery and cinematography, an impending sense of doom, melancholy, and tense sequences that will jar your stomach for days to come.

Whereas "Rakka" implemented a survivalist nature with its human characters, "Firebase" focuses on the deep, underlining guilt that plagues the topic of the Vietnam War. The philosophy in "Firebase" is handled well, while also combining mythological themes with authentic locations and events. Blomkamp has never been afraid to tread waters that most would find daunting, and he proves to have made the right decision in challenging himself to present such a multi-faceted and morose tale of guilt and retribution.

OUR RATING: 4/5 STARS

PART 3: ZYGOTE

The last installment of our review series on director Neill Blomkamp's OATS Studios short films–at least until a new short releases–will revolve around "Zygote." An abomination of John Carpenter's The Thing and the video game franchise Dead Space, with a dabble of Event Horizon, "Zygote" is horrifying and grotesque in the most perfect of ways. Blomkamp yet again secures and executes an interesting idea and in doing so, maintains a consistent level of quality to be expected from his passion project.

"Zygote" follows two humans on a terraforming station who are trying to survive from the pursuit of an otherworldy creature that not only absorbs all knowledge from each person it encounters, but it also literally absorbs and combines every human it kills, making its physical appearance disturbing and visceral. Audiences are kind of thrown into the mix, initially unaware, and we have to listen to everything the two characters say in order to grasp a better understanding of the universe and environment. Blomkamp has stated that this storyline was originally thought up to be a full length film, which makes sense if you consider how deep this storyline actually runs.

Where the film could drastically fail, considering its lack of setup, Blomkamp masterfully keeps the audience engaged with exposition scenes that cohesively fill the absences in narrative. Once the short picks up, and once we see the Zygote (and hear it) for the first time, the film is nonstop terror from then on. The creature is frightening and jarring in its unnatural resemblance to humans alone. The CGI could have gone terribly wrong with this concept, but surprisingly, the Zygote looks better in this level of quality CGI than it would have in practical effects, which is an enormous compliment to the crew who worked on this film.

The Carpenter and Cronenberg themes culminate into a tense and horrific ending that does not disappoint, even with our clamoring to see a prelude to these events. This was a very interesting theme and concept to see Blomkamp tackle, as his work has primarily been in the realms of hard science fiction. Seeing him so flawlessly execute a sci-fi/horror like "Zygote" is impressive in its determinations of his skill alone. Not only does Blomkamp deliver with a gripping short, but he also crafts what is the best short film in OATS Studios Volume 1 thus far. "Zygote" is exactly what it needs to be, never failing to remember its purpose or design.

OUR RATING: 5/5 STARS

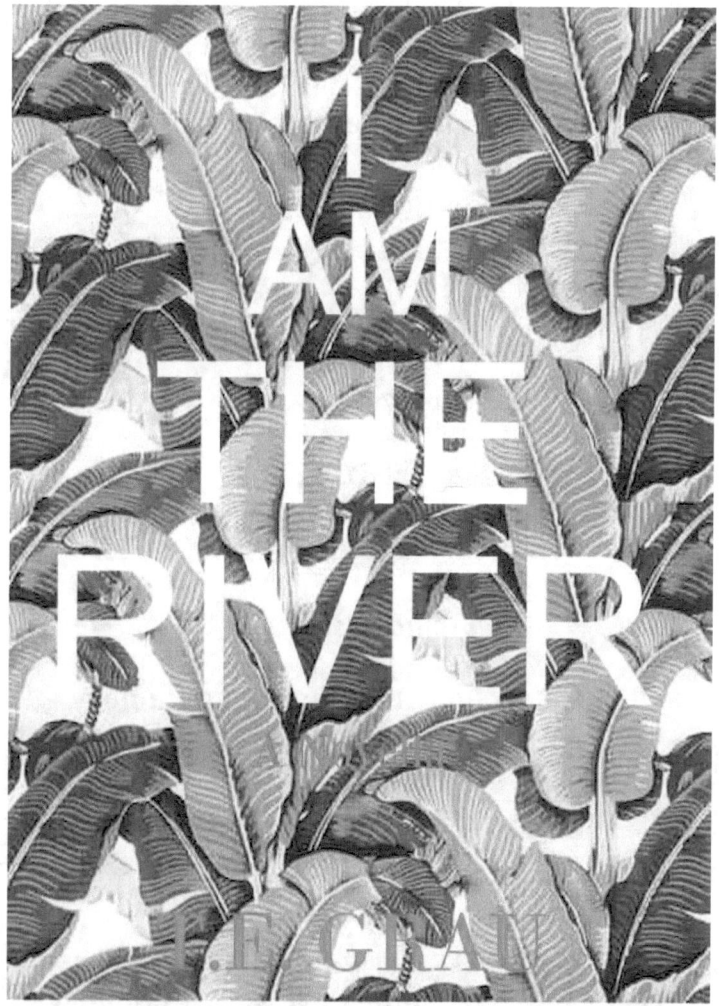

If you enjoyed **Hinnom Magazine**, make sure to leave a review on Amazon and follow us on social media!

Facebook: www.facebook.com/gehennaandhinnom-books
Twitter: www.twitter.com/GehennaBooks
Website: www.gehennaandhinnom.wordpress.com

Look out for our releases in 2017!

June 30th, 2017

Hinnom Magazine Issue 001

August 31st, 2017

Hinnom Magazine Issue 002

September 30th, 2017

Year's Best Body Horror 2017 Anthology

October 31st, 2017

Hinnom Magazine Issue 003

November 30th, 2017

Year's Best Transhuman SF 2017 Anthology

December 31st, 2017

Hinnom Magazine Issue 004

www.ingramcontent.com/pod-product-compliance
Lightning Source LLC
Chambersburg PA
CBHW050930120626
46552CB00001B/140